MW00577696

A Merry Masquerade For Christmas

La Petite Mort Club, Volume 4

Ellis O. Day

Published by LSODea, 2018.

Copyright © 2018 Ellis O. Day
All rights reserved.
ISBN-13 978-1-942706-36-6
PRINT ISBN-13: 9781393119920

All rights reserved. This book or any portion thereof may not be reproduced or used
in any manner whatsoever without the express written permission of the publisher
except for the use of brief quotations in a book review.

This is a work of fiction. Names, characters, businesses, places, events and incidents
are either the products of the author's imagination or used in a fictitious manner.
Any resemblance to actual persons, living or dead, or actual events is purely
coincidental.

I love to hear from readers so email me at
authorellisoday@gmail.com
http://www.EllisODay.com
Facebook
https://www.facebook.com/EllisODayRomanceAuthor/
Closed FB Group
https://www.facebook.com/groups/153238782143373

Twitter
https://twitter.com/ellis_o_day

Pinterest
www.pinterest.com\AuthorEllisODay

Also by Ellis O. Day

The Dom's Submission
His Sub
His Mission
His Submission

The Voyeur
The Voyeur
Watching the Voyeur
Touching the Voyeur
Loving the Voyeur

CHAPTER 1: LIZ

Elizabeth sat in the office of La Petite Mort Club, trying not to stare. The owner, Ethan St. Johns, was the sexiest man she'd ever seen. Yes, he was good looking with his strong cheek bones and sandy brown hair, but it was more than that. There was something about him that made her want to be bad.

"So, Mrs. White, are you sure you want to join La Petite Mort Club." Ethan's blue eyes searched her face.

"Yes." She struggled to remain passive under his perusal. She wasn't going to admit that the only reason she wanted to join the sex club was because her husband was a member.

"Who recommended us to you?"

"No one."

"Please, Mrs. White. Someone must have pointed you to us. We don't run ads in the neighborhood flyer." He smiled and she swore her knees actually melted.

"Of course not." She giggled. This was ridiculous. She was a grown woman, mother of three adult children, not a teenage girl with her first crush. She cleared her throat. "I heard about this place...through a friend." She'd thought her husband was her best friend until she'd found the membership card in his dresser drawer.

Even though she'd understood the French name, she'd had to Google the place. She hadn't truly believed that Craig had been cheating on her, but he had and not only with one woman but a club full of young women. She'd died a little that day.

"And who might this friend be?" He leaned back in his seat. "I'll be honest, Mrs. White. I'm not inclined to grant membership to just anyone."

"I'm not just anyone."

1

"You're not our typical client."

"Because I'm not male?" She should've figured as much. Men her age were considered distinguished whereas women—no matter how much they stayed in shape or colored their hair—were old.

"Because you're married."

She glanced at her hand but the ring was gone. She'd lost a little more of her heart when she'd taken it off, knowing it was never going back on her finger. "My husband. I found out about this place through my husband."

"Really?" He seemed genuinely surprised.

"Yes." She never would've known this vile place existed if not for his infidelity.

"In that case, you don't need to fill out any paperwork. You can have Craig add you to his membership." He leaned forward as if to stand, as if this meeting was over.

"No." She didn't want her husband knowing anything about this until he saw her here.

"It's less expensive."

"I don't care about the money." That wasn't their problem anymore. She almost wished it were.

They'd been a team while struggling to make ends meet, but once his advertising business had taken off, she'd quit her job to take care of the kids. Now, the children were grown and gone and she was alone.

"I see." He smiled softly. "May I ask why you don't want Craig to know about this?"

"That's not..." The look on his face told her not to bother lying. "We're getting divorced."

"Oh." Again he seemed surprised. "I'm sorry to hear that."

"Yes. Well..." She wasn't sure what to say when people said that because she was sorry too. She still loved her husband, but he didn't feel the same.

"This poses a problem." Ethan steepled his hands in front of him.

"Why?"

"It isn't my policy to allow divorced couples to both be members."

"What? Because he's a member, I can't be?"

"Sorry, but yes."

"Why?" She wanted to scream it wasn't fair—just like him cheating on her wasn't fair—but she was pretty sure throwing a tantrum wasn't the way to get through to this man.

He shrugged. "Fighting—real fighting, not play fighting—isn't the atmosphere I want at the Club. This is a place for men and women to get away from their troubles, not find them."

"So now, I'm Craig's trouble." She'd had about enough. This was all Craig's fault. He was the one who'd cheated. The one who'd stopped wanting her.

"I didn't say that...exactly."

"It's fine. I can join another Club." There had to be other ones, but she wanted to be here. She wanted Craig to see that at forty-five she was still an attractive, desirable, sexual woman.

"I can recommend a few." He leaned forward, opening his desk drawer.

"No. Don't." She stood. "I'll call my lawyer instead."

"Your lawyer?" He stared up at her, a hardness in his blue eyes.

"I believe your practices are discriminatory."

"Do you?" He relaxed in his chair. "This is a private club and I can choose who I accept. I have not discriminated against you because of your gender, religion, race or because you are of a...certain age."

She looked away. She would not cry. She wasn't twenty or thirty but forty-five wasn't old.

"Sit, please." He stood.

She sat. She had no idea why but there was something about him that made her obey.

"Let me get you something to drink."

"No, thank you. I'm fine." As fine as any woman who still loved her cheating husband could be. Twenty-three years of marriage gone. Thrown away.

"Wine? White, red or rose?"

"Red please." She may as well have a drink. If she were nice, maybe she could persuade Ethan to grant her a membership. Eventually, she'd get over this betrayal, but right now, she needed Craig to feel something for her. If she couldn't have his love or desire, she'd take his anger.

He walked to the bar and poured a glass of wine. He came back to the desk and handed it to her.

"Thank you."

He sat. "Now, Mrs. White—"

"Elizabeth. Liz."

He nodded. "Elizabeth, please tell me why you really want a membership."

She took a sip of her wine. Telling him the truth wouldn't work, but she was pretty sure he'd see through her lie. So, half-truth it was, no matter how embarrassing. "I want to have sex."

"That goes without saying." He grinned. "This is La Petite Mort Club."

She'd expected some reaction but she shouldn't have. Everyone who joined wanted that. She took a deep breath. "I want to feel desirable again, wanted."

"And your husband doesn't do this for you?"

She shook her head, her throat too tight to speak.

"Hmm." He steepled his fingers again, studying her.

"That can't be unusual for women...couples my age." Age had never bothered her until now—until Craig had turned to another woman or women...younger women.

"It isn't but it is unusual for the woman to want to join the same establishment as her husband." He leaned closer to her. "That usually only happens if she wants him back or wants to teach him a lesson. Neither of those reasons are welcome in my club."

"That's not it. Truly." She was losing ground. "I...this is the only place that I know of—"

"I offered to give you names of similar clubs."

"Yes, but this one...Craig trusts it, so I do too. I don't want to catch something or...or get hurt."

He studied her for a long moment. "You truly want to do this? Join the Club and have sex with strangers?"

"Is it that hard to believe a woman in her forties wants sex? I'm sure most of your male clientele are my age or older."

"It's hard to believe this of you."

"Me? You don't even know me."

He opened his desk drawer and pulled out a manila folder. "I do background checks on all potential customers."

"You....you looked into my past." Not that she had anything to hide. She and Craig had met and started dating in college. They'd married shortly after graduation and she'd gotten pregnant right away. They'd had three wonderful children and she'd thought a great life, but obviously, it and she hadn't been enough for him.

"Yes and you don't seem the type to want to fuck strange men."

She stiffened at the obscenity and he smirked. "Well, I'm changing. Divorce can do that to a woman."

"It can do that to a man too."

"Are you divorced?"

He laughed. "No. Never been married."

"Then you have no idea." No idea of the devastation, the betrayal, the emptiness inside—the place her husband had filled was now a hollow, empty cavern.

"I've seen more married and divorced couples in their most basic element than you ever will. I'm quite familiar with people and their games."

Good thing he hadn't said women and their games. She might've had to slap him. "I'm sure you are, but I'm not playing games of any kind." She needed to stick to her story. Any deviation would be her downfall.

"You're telling me that you and Craig are parting amicably?"

"Yes." Not exactly, but that didn't matter.

"Good." He closed the folder. "I'll call him and make sure he's okay with me giving you a membership."

"You can't do that." She wanted to surprise Craig, to shock him, and telling him ahead of time wouldn't accomplish that.

"That's the only way you're getting inside this Club."

"Fine. I'll go somewhere else." She stood and strode to the door. Men were all assholes.

CHAPTER 2: CRAIG

Craig sat at his desk, staring out his office window. This couldn't be happening, but it was. The papers on his desk didn't lie. Liz wanted a divorce. He'd thought they were happy—that she was happy. Sure, their sex life wasn't as good as he would've liked, but he'd hoped now that the kids were gone they could work on that. She wouldn't be so tired all the time and they could be more spontaneous. None of that was going to happen because she wanted out. After twenty-three good years of marriage—or at least he'd thought they were good—she was done with their family, with him.

There was a knock on his door and Ben, one of his employees, peeked his head in.

"What do you want?" Craig quickly wiped his eyes.

"Were you crying?"

"No. Allergies." He wasn't ready to tell anyone about the divorce.

"I thought you went to the doctor for that?"

"I did." And it'd caused the worst few months of his life—his eyes dropped to the papers on his desk—until now.

"Maybe, you should go back. You don't look too good."

"I'm fine. What do you want?"

"Oh, I need to borrow your car."

"Again?" This was the third time in less than two months."

"Yeah. Sorry."

His phone rang. He pulled his keys from his pocket and tossed them to Ben. "Get a new car and close the door behind you." He grabbed his phone. "Hello."

"Craig White?" asked a man.

"You called my office." He should be polite. This could be a potential customer but right now, he didn't care.

The man laughed. "Yes, I know but I wanted to make sure it was you."

"Who is this?"

"Sorry. This is Ethan St. Johns."

"Who?"

"From La Petite Mort Club."

"Oh, Ethan. Right." He glanced at the door to ensure it was closed. "How are things? Everything okay with the ad team I have working for you?"

"Yes. Ben and Gabby are fantastic and I love the new materials."

"Great. Glad to hear it." Ethan had been one of his first big-money clients.

Initially, he'd found the idea of producing ad copy for a sex club distasteful, but then he'd met Ethan. The younger man had insisted on giving him a tour. The place was clean, respectable and everyone was there because they wanted to be, not because they had to.

He took a shaky breath, trying to air out the sadness in his voice. "Then, how can I help you."

"Actually, I think I may be able to help you...or this may not help at all."

"What are you talking about?" There was an edge to Ethan's voice that made him nervous.

"I'm not sure how to tell you this, so I'll just say it. Your wife came to visit me today."

"She did what?" His hand clutched the phone so tightly he was surprised it didn't break. Liz had gone to a sex club? Impossible. No. No way.

"She'd filled out an application online to join and I asked her—"

"She did what?" He was repeating himself but his brain wasn't functioning correctly. Neither were his ears. "She wanted to join your club? Your sex club?"

"Yes." There was a hint of amusement in Ethan's tone.

"This isn't funny." Not only did the woman he loved—the mother of his children—not want him to touch her anymore, but she wanted to fuck and god know what else with strange men.

"Of course not." Ethan's tone was somber but Craig knew the other man was humoring him.

"You're mistaken about this. It's not possible. My Liz..." But she wasn't his Liz any more.

"I thought it was a mistake too. White isn't an uncommon last name. So, I called and asked her to come to my office. That way, I could see if perhaps this was a different woman with the same name, but it wasn't."

"How do you know my wife?" Ethan was young and good looking. He didn't want Liz anywhere near the man.

"I researched you before I offered you my account."

"You ran a background check on me *and* my family?" He wanted to hang up, go over there and beat the guy senseless.

"Yes. I couldn't have just anyone representing me and my business. You understand." Ethan's tone was calm and soothing. Professional.

Craig's temper eased. It made sense. Ethan's business was sensitive.

"It was your wife...soon to be ex-wife who came to my office."

"She told you about the divorce." His gaze dropped to the papers on his desk.

"Yes, and I'm sorry."

"Me too." He hadn't meant to say it. It'd just slipped out.

"I refused her membership."

"Good. Thank you." There was no way Liz was going to a place like that.

"I'm not sure it is good."

"Excuse me." He actually took the phone away from his face and stared at it.

"She mentioned something about finding a different club."

"What?" He shot to his feet, pressing the phone to his ear.

"That's why I called. Some of the other places are...less than reputable. I tried giving her a list—"

"You did what?" He was back to wanting to punch the other man.

"There are some other clubs that are good. Not as good as mine, of course, but they are safe."

"She is not joining a sex club."

"Okay, but...How are you going to stop her?"

"I..." That was a good question. She wasn't going to listen to him. She didn't even want to be around him.

"I have a suggestion."

"You do?" He dropped back onto his chair.

"Yes, but first, I have to ask you some personal questions."

"Like what?" Personal questions from a man like Ethan could get a lot more personal than he was willing to go.

"About your marriage."

"That's none of your business."

"You're right. It isn't but I may be able to help."

"How can you help my marriage?"

"Why don't you come by after work and we can talk?"

"We can talk now."

"It might be better with a drink."

"Then pour me a rum and coke. Easy on the coke." He grabbed the divorce papers and stood. "I'm on my way."

CHAPTER 3: CRAIG

By the time Craig arrived at La Petite Mort Club he was ready to kill Liz. How dare she want to join a sex club. She never even wanted to have sex, not with him, and that was the part that destroyed him.

He paid the Uber driver and headed toward the building. Their life hadn't been perfect but it'd been pretty damn good—their sex life too or at least he'd thought so. He hesitated at the door to the Club, the sex club. That's what she wanted. Sex with a man...men other than him. His knees almost buckled. God, this hurt more than he'd ever admit. Screw her. If she wanted out, he'd let her go. Let her fuck every man she found. She'd never find anyone who'd treat her like he had.

He'd made a good home for them. A good life. They didn't need money. They had their health. What more did she want? *Another man's dick, that's what she wanted.* He threw the door open and stepped inside.

The bouncer, obviously expecting him, didn't even get up from the table. "Welcome, Mr. White. Ethan said you know the way to his office."

"I do. Thanks." He'd jogged up the stairs. He'd spent many hours here when he'd first gotten the account. Ethan had even given him a complimentary membership so he could come and go as he wanted.

He sighed as he stopped at the door that led to the back offices. He'd found that old card while cleaning out the closet a few months back. He'd almost shown it to Liz. He'd wanted to suggest that they visit when Robbie, their youngest, left for college but since he'd never told her anything about the Club, he'd decided it was better not to mention it. Maybe, he should've. Things couldn't have gone any worse.

A buzzer sounded and he opened the door, walking into the hallway that led to the back offices and the staff quarters. This area was as sparse and business like as the public rooms were elegantly opulent. He preferred this section. He was successful and wealthy but he'd rather a night around a camp fire with a few good friends than an evening of decadence.

He stopped at Ethan's office, raising his hand to knock when the door opened.

"Craig, good to see you." Ethan smiled and stepped aside so he could enter. "Sorry it had to be on these terms."

"Yeah." He went into the office. A bottle of Bacardi, a two-liter of Coke and a bucket of ice sat on the table in front of the couch.

"Please, have a seat." Ethan closed the door and sat down in a chair across from the couch. He picked up his snifter of brandy from the nearby end table.

"The Club looks good, as always." It was a clean, classic and elegant establishment. He sat on the couch, picking up the Barcardi and pouring a hefty amount in the glass before adding ice and a splash of Coke.

"Thanks. Redecorated a few years ago. Probably time to do it again." Ethan watched him as he tossed back the rum and coke and poured another.

He coughed. He didn't imbibe much and he never drank anything as strong as he'd made that drink. He made an identical one. If he were going to tell the other man to let his wife have access to the Club so she could fuck every man here, he needed to be plastered.

"I'm sorry to hear about the divorce."

"Yeah." He added a little Coke and took another gulp. Drunk was fine but there was no reason to poison himself. That'd make Liz way too happy.

"May I ask what happened?"

"What difference does it make? My wife wants out." He had no idea what'd happened. He tossed back the entire drink. "She wants to fuck other men."

"Are you sure about that?"

"I have the divorce papers and you told me she wants to join your club. Don't need numbers to connect those dots.

"I don't think she wants to join because she wants to fuck other men."

"Why else would she want to come here?" He topped off his glass with more rum. "No offense."

"None taken." Ethan grinned. "Actually, I'd be offended if you didn't think that. This is the top sex club in the states and the men and women here are extremely fuckable."

"Shut up. I don't want to hear about my competition." Replacement was more accurate.

"You still love her?"

"Of course, I still love her."

"Okay, but do you want to fuck her?" Ethan eyes were a brilliant blue.

"What does it matter?" He had some pride. Ethan knew she didn't want him.

"It makes all the difference in the world."

"Really? How do you figure that? She wants a divorce. She doesn't want me." So much for his pride.

"Answer my question and I'll explain."

He tossed back his drink and refilled it. They were finally starting to taste good. "Yes, I still want her."

"You want to fuck her?"

"That's what I said."

"No, you said you wanted her."

"Same thing."

"Hmm. I suppose."

"What are you getting at?"

"Like I said, I don't believe your wife wants to come here to fuck other men." He held up his hand to stop Craig from interrupting. "I believe she wants you to see her."

"She wants me to see her fucking other men." He stood. He didn't need this shit. "Fine. Give her a membership. Actually, give her mine. I don't use it anyway." He was going to buy a bottle, go to his apartment and forget everything. Had he ever been enough for her? How many years had she been pretending to care, pretending to want to make love with him? Had she been imagining other men and dreaming of the day she could leave him?

"Sit down. She doesn't want you to see her fucking other men. She wants you to see her as a woman. As a desirable woman."

"I do." He dropped back onto the couch. "She's the sexiest woman I know."

"Does she know this?"

"Of course, she does. Until she accused me of cheating—which I have *never* done—and kicked me out, we still made love."

"How often? You don't need to answer me but I want you to be honest with yourself." Ethan finished his drink and walked to the bar across the room.

Their sex life had been...average. Over the years, life had gotten in the way. He was always working or she was busy or tired. They just didn't do it that often. He'd hoped that with the kids gone, they could work on that, but it was never going to happen now.

Ethan came back and sat down, refilled snifter in his hand. "Your wife thinks you don't want her anymore."

"She said that?"

"Yes."

"That's a lie. I try...She's never in the mood." The last few times he'd suggested sex, she'd turned him down flat.

"Perhaps, you should try harder."

"She wants a divorce. If I try now, I'll get arrested."

"I think, she still loves you."

"Really?" He shouldn't care what Ethan thought but his heart wanted to believe those words.

"Yeah. I suggested other clubs but she wasn't interested. She wanted to join my club because you'd be here."

"But I don't come here." When he'd first gotten the account years ago, he'd visited in the early evenings a lot. He had to get the feel for the place so he could promote it, but once he'd gotten his idea for the campaign, he hadn't gone into the actual Club part of the business again.

"I know, but you're missing the point. She knows about your membership."

"How?" Shit, that wasn't good.

"She said you told her."

"Me?" He pointed to his chest. "No." He shook his head. "No way. Why would I do that?"

"I don't know. Maybe you mentioned it when you first landed the account?" Ethan took a sip of his drink.

"I was going to. I thought we could celebrate the extra money but she'd just found out that her sister's husband was cheating and...I decided it was better not to mention it." He dropped his head in his hands. "I don't know how she found out, but I should've told her. I was going to later, but..."

"She would've wondered why you hadn't told her right away."

"Exactly. She'd would've assumed I didn't tell her because I had been coming here and I had but not for that."

"Precisely what she assumes now."

"But how did she find out?"

"I have no idea, but she definitely knows." Ethan took a sip of his drink, studying the other man. "She also said that it wouldn't be a problem if you saw her here. That your divorce was amicable."

"Amicable? She served me with the papers last week."

"And did you fight with her?"

"No. I called and she was upset and I...I didn't want to make it worse."

"Perhaps, you should've fought with her about it."

"She was crying." He hated when she cried.

"Women do that." Ethan leaned forward. "Maybe, she wanted you to fight for her. To prove that you weren't going to let her go so easily."

"She should know how I feel. We've been together since college." And it was all over. God, the hole in his chest was so deep and dark he could fall inside and never come out. She'd done this to him. Her. He hadn't done anything to deserve this.

"Maybe she should but she doesn't."

"How in the fuck do you know what she feels? I've been married to her forever and I didn't see this coming, but you meet her once..."

"Before you accuse me of anything, yes, I have only met her once." One side of Ethan's mouth curved upward. "And I know, because I know people. It's my business. I've seen people wearing all kinds of masks, figuratively and literally. Your wife's choice of mask is indifference with a touch of anger, but beneath that is nothing but sadness and hurt."

"Hurt? Her? She's the one doing this. She hurt me." He tossed back his drink and slammed the glass on the table. His fingers fumbled with the rum bottle almost knocking it over.

Ethan grabbed it.

"Fill 'er up." He tapped his glass.

"I'll need your keys if you want any more," said Ethan.

He laughed. "I'd happily give them to you, but I didn't drive."

"What?"

"Ben's car broke down."

"Again? You need to pay the guy more."

"I pay him plenty." He tapped his glass. He was so close to beautiful inebriation. He didn't want to let it slip away.

"Then tell him to get a new car. I have a lot of events planned and I can't have him breaking down and missing them." Ethan poured a hefty amount of rum in the glass.

"Ben does like the perks of his membership." He tossed in some ice.

"He's a good guy." Ethan added a splash of Coke.

"Yep, but his car sucks."

"Speaking of events. We're having a masked Christmas Eve party," said Ethan.

"That's great." He tried to sound enthused but failed. He'd be alone. Robbie was going skiing with friends. Tina was spending this Christmas at her fiancé's parents and Ellie was working. He'd thought it'd just be him and Liz but now he'd be alone and she'd be fucking someone—maybe even here.

"It is, especially if you want to seduce your wayward wife."

"What?" His eyes snapped to Ethan's.

"I can send an invite to her. Make it look like a mistake and you can be here."

"With her?" He didn't think she'd let him take her anywhere, let alone a sex club.

"Not with her. Pick her up. Seduce her."

"Here?" He wasn't a bad looking guy but there were some exceptionally good looking men and woman at this place and many of them were younger than he was.

"Yes. It's the perfect place. Are you seeing her for Christmas?"

"No. She's filed for divorce, remember?"

"You won't see your kids?"

"They're all busy. None are coming into town."

"Perfect. Find a reason to see her or at least to talk to her. Mention...No, let it slip that you have plans Christmas Eve. She'll be expecting you to be here."

"Why would she expect me to be here?"

"Maybe, you should slow down on the drinking. This isn't that complicated," said Ethan. "She thinks you frequent this place, remember?"

"Oh. That's right." He grinned and took another drink, but then frowned. "Your plan isn't going to work."

"And why not?" Ethan seemed offended.

"She'll be pissed when she sees me here. I'll be lucky if she talks to me, let alone lets me take her home." And he couldn't handle seeing her with another man. Not now. Not ever.

"She won't see *you*."

"What?" This wasn't making sense. Maybe, Ethan was right. He put his drink down.

"The masks remember? It's a masked party."

"Oh." That made sense but..."What if I don't recognize her?"

"She has to show her invitation to enter. I'll have the bouncer notify me when she arrives and I'll point her out to you."

"Oh...okay. That'd work." Could he do this? What if she turned him down. What if she picked some other guy? "What if she recognizes me?"

"She won't. Wear different cologne."

"My voice."

"Don't talk too much and when you do, try to speak in a lower tone." Ethan grinned. "Get her into one of the rooms as soon as possible and make her scream. Then, you can let her know it's you and that you still want her and can still make her beg."

"I can do that. I can definitely do that." He finished another drink. "I'll fuck her until she can't stand." He was going to prove to his wife that his was the only dick she needed or wanted.

CHAPTER 4: LIZ

"I love you too, Robbie." Liz struggled to keep the sadness from her voice. "Yes, I'm sure. Go and have fun with your friends. I'll be fine and so will your father. Yes, call me on Christmas."

As soon as she hung up, she let the tears fall. This was going to be the worst Christmas ever. She'd never been alone on Christmas. Never. She stared at the tree—all decked out with lights and ornaments, memories of better times. She shouldn't have bothered putting it up. With the kids gone and Craig...out of her life, there'd been no reason, except she'd thought it'd make her feel better. Sometimes, it did—when she was busy in the kitchen or at her desk working—but not now. Not when Christmas was only a few days away and she was going to be miserable by herself.

She'd imagined their first Christmas without the kids. She'd snuggle alongside Craig on the couch in the dark, no lights but those from the tree. He'd see her as more than his wife and the mother of his children. He'd see her as he once had years ago, as a woman, one he desired. She missed him—his voice, his laughter, his touch—but she had to remember that he wasn't worth missing. He was a cheating bastard.

All those nights, him claiming to work late and her being so gullible, tore into her stomach. She'd actually felt bad for him, putting in all those hours for her and the kids. God, she was an idiot. She'd never suspected that he was cheating, let alone frequenting a sex club. She hated that place but more than that she hated Craig for doing this to them. Their life hadn't been perfect but she'd love it and him. They could've worked through their issues, anything but cheating. That she couldn't forgive—ever.

Her phone rang. She looked at the screen. *Think of the devil.* "What?" She was in no mood to be polite.

"I guess you still have me in caller id." Craig was pissed.

Too bad. It wasn't her job to make him feel good or special any more. "Did you call to check?"

"No."

She waited. She hoped he'd apologize. Beg her to forgive him, but he wouldn't. He wasn't the apologizing kind of guy. "You did want something, right?"

"Are you okay?" His voice was soft with concern.

"Of course." It was so tempting to fall into that familiar voice, to let him hold her, comfort her, but she couldn't do that. He'd hurt her too much. "Why wouldn't I be?"

"It's Christmas. The kids are gone." He didn't say it. He didn't have to, but they both knew what was hiding under those words—he was gone too and she was alone.

"Yes, I'm quite aware of all that." And that he'd cheated on her. That he'd slept with women instead of her. That he'd stopped wanting her but, damn her heart, she hadn't stopped wanting him.

"I was thinking that since we're both—"

"Don't. Please. Just don't." Her voice cracked and she coughed, trying lamely to cover her tears. She was weak right now. If he offered to come over, she'd take him back and nothing would change.

"Okay." His voice was hard now, filled with hurt or anger.

Good because she was both and he deserved to feel some of that too.

"I thought, I could stop by Christmas day and we could have breakfast together. Like we used to."

"I...I don't think that's a good idea." She wanted to say yes—be granted a temporary reprieve from this sadness and pain. Unfortunately, she didn't think she was strong enough to kick him out again and she wouldn't live with a man she couldn't trust.

"Right." He was pissed again. "I'm stopping by tomorrow."

"Craig—"

"You don't have to be there."

"You're not coming over unless I'm here." She clutched the phone tighter. This was her home. She deserved it. She hadn't destroyed their marriage.

"It's still my house too, Liz."

"Well, you're not living here anymore."

"And whose fault is that? It certainly isn't mine."

"Oh, that's rich. Because you had nothing to do with this"—she waved her hand around—"mess between us." Her voice broke.

"It's my fault?" He was almost yelling now. "I'm not the one who decided to file for divorce. I'm not—"

"I'm not going to argue with you about this again." She took a deep breath. He'd denied and denied cheating. She'd even started to believe him, until she'd seen his car at La Petite Mort Club.

"Fine. I'm coming over tomorrow. I'd prefer you not be there."

"Why are you coming over?"

He took a deep breath. "You don't want to be my wife anymore, so I don't have to tell you shit."

"Like you ever did."

"I told you everything."

"You lied about everything."

"God damnit." It sounded like he moved the phone away from his face as he mumbled.

"What do you need? Maybe, I can find it and have it ready so we don't have to go through this again."

"The Halloween stuff."

"What? Why do you need that?"

"I just do."

"It's a bunch of old costumes that I should've thrown away years ago."

"I'm glad you didn't."

"What do you want out of there?" Neither of them had ever never been into Halloween like some adults.

"That's none of your business."

"You're being an ass." That hurt, especially because it was true.

"And you're being a bitch."

She inhaled sharply. Craig cussed but he never directed it at her. That was her flaw.

"Have it ready, or don't. I'll find it myself. Either way, I don't care."

He hung up the phone.

CHAPTER 5: CRAIG

Craig pulled into his driveway. He loved their house. It was modest in size but well-made but more than that, it was home. A heaviness settled on his shoulders and in his chest, making him feel older than his forty-eight years. He didn't want a divorce. He didn't want to date again. He wanted his wife.

Liz stepped out of the house and he let his eyes roam over her. God, he loved this woman. She didn't look much different than the day they'd met over twenty years ago. Her hips had widened and her breasts weren't as firm, but it didn't detract from her looks. Instead, it made her look like the woman she was, not the young girl she'd been. Her hair was lighter now—more a honey blonde than brown—but it suited her. He hardened at the memory of how soft it was cascading over his chest, and the smell—fuck, she always smelled so fresh and warm, like lemons with vanilla.

"Did you come here to sit in the driveway?" She gave him the look she usually saved for the kids when they disappointed her.

He didn't deserve that look. He hadn't done anything wrong. He opened the door and got out. "Morning."

"Good morning." She headed for the garage which was already open. "The Halloween boxes are in here."

"Yeah, I figured as much." Apparently, she didn't want him going through the house. It was his goddamn house too.

She pulled down the ladder to the attic, her jeans slipping down her hips and showing a tiny bit of the soft skin along her belly. He wanted to drop to his knees and kiss it—trail his tongue along that velvety smoothness, feeling her heat and tasting the salt on her skin. She tugged up her pants and climbed the ladder, knocking him from his fantasies.

"I can get them." He moved to the ladder.

"I'll hand them to you." Her top half was already in the ceiling.

She'd lost some weight. Was it due to the stress of their divorce or was she trying to drop a few pounds for some other guy? He wanted to beat this nameless guy senseless. She stretched, her ass wiggling in front of his face. His hands itched to touch her—to skim over the round cheeks and then down her hips to her thighs. If she turned around her pussy would be even with his lips. His pants were getting uncomfortably tight. He was dying for her and she wanted someone else. Correction. She wanted anyone else.

"Here." She turned, handing him a box, not noticing when his eyes continued to stare at the juncture between her thighs—the one place he most wanted to be in the world.

"Craig, it's kind of heavy."

She didn't even see him as a man anymore. His jaw clenched as he took the box and walked across the room, dropping it on the cabinet.

"Do you want me to get the other ones or do you want to check that one first?"

"Let me look in this one." He couldn't stand that close to her ass another moment without touching her, kissing her. With the mood she was in lately, that'd land him in jail.

He opened the box. On top was the Power Ranger costume Tina had loved. Memories washed over him—all the Halloweens and Christmases, birthdays, sick days and summers. He missed his life. It'd been filled with laughter and love and it was all gone.

"Is it in there?"

He clutched the pink costume, his throat too tight for words.

"If you tell me what you're looking for I may be able to help."

"I got it." Stuffed on the side of the box was a black domino mask. It'd do. Ethan would give him a different one anyway. He forced himself to put the Power Ranger costume back, grab the mask and close the box. He carried it over and handed it to her. "Thanks for helping."

"You wanted a mask?" She stared at his hand, not taking the box.

"Yeah." By the pinched look on her face, Ethan was right. This was driving her crazy.

"Why do you need a mask? Are you going to rob a bank?" She joked but not knowing was killing her.

"Not exactly." He shook the box a little. "Do you want me to put it away?"

"No. I got it." She took it from him and turned.

His eyes went to her ass again. He'd always loved her butt. It was firm and round and her skin was so soft.

She started down the steps. He should back away, give her some room but his legs wouldn't move. If he touched her, maybe, they could get past this...mistake, misunderstanding. Whatever it was that was destroying their marriage.

She turned, brushing against him. His eyes locked with her brown ones and there was passion there, flickering in the dark depths.

"Liz." He had to kiss her. He had to show her how much he wanted her, how much she still wanted him.

"Don't." She turned her head and stepped away.

His hand tightened on the damn mask, ready to rip it in two.

"Ah...did you need anything else?" She stood at the garage door as if dismissing him.

He almost said a fucking explanation on why she didn't love him anymore.

"A gun maybe?" She smiled and it was like she tore out his heart. She had the best smile—wide and friendly and her eyes always sparkled with mischief.

"No." He tried to smile back but couldn't. "This will do it."

"A mask...for Christmas?"

"Christmas Eve." He corrected.

"You need a mask for Christmas Eve? Why would you...You're going out on Christmas Eve? Who goes out on Christmas Eve?"

"Single people, Liz. You know. People who don't want to be alone. People like me." He strode over to her. "We're the people who go out. We go to parties and we do this so we can forget our fucking families. You know, the ones who don't want us anymore." He stormed to his car because if he didn't get out of there right now he was going to grab her and never let her go—or at least hold her until the cops arrived.

CHAPTER 6: CRAIG

Craig called Ethan. "I got a mask and told her I was going to a party on Christmas Eve. She was not very happy."

"Perfect. I'll send her the text message tomorrow."

"You have her number?" Why would Ethan have her number?

"It was on the application." Ethan's tone was amused.

"Right. Sorry." He wanted to throttle her for even thinking about going to a place like that.

"Get a haircut, a new suit and new cologne. I'll supply the mask. Oh, and come early. I'll let you know when she arrives."

"Got it and....thanks."

"Anytime."

He hung up the phone and picked up his divorce papers. He tore them in half. He was not losing the only woman he'd ever loved. He was going to prove to her that she still wanted him. That she still loved him. He tossed the papers into the trash and left to get his hair cut.

CHAPTER 7: LIZ

Liz shoved the mop across the floor. She always cleaned when she was upset. Her house was going to be spotless. This was all so unfair and so typical. Craig was going to a party—a masked party on Christmas Eve. She'd be sitting home, crying and watching *It's a Wonderful Life,* while her husband would be having the time of his life, fucking some whore. She snorted. Nothing new there. He'd been doing it for years.

Her phone beeped. That'd better not be him needing something else. She'd skewer him with the mop handle if she had to see him again.

She put the mop down and walked into the kitchen to grab her phone. Damn, he'd looked good yesterday—his body strong and lean, his dark brown hair a little too long. When she'd turned and he'd been looking at her with desire...no hot lust, she'd almost fallen into his arms. She hated that she still wanted the bastard. He'd never change. He'd always cheat—her father had, her sister's husband had. Craig wouldn't be any different, especially with a membership to that club. God, she hated that place. Even the name made her skin crawl. The little death. Yes, it meant orgasm but for her it meant the death of her marriage.

She grabbed her phone off the counter and stared at her messages. This had to be a mistake, but it wasn't. It was a blessing.

Come (in every way imaginable) and check out La Petite Mort's Happy Endings Christmas Eve Bash. Mask Required. Clothing Optional. Doors open at 6 pm. Non-members show this message for entry.

This had to be the party Craig was attending. Ethan must've forgotten to remove her from the potential client list. It was her own Christmas miracle. She hurried to the garage. She had to find a mask. She was going to show Craig that she wasn't just his wife—soon to be ex-wife. She was a woman who needed a man and she was still attractive enough to get one.

CHAPTER 8: LIZ

Liz parked her car in the lot outside La Petite Mort Club as a group of four people walked toward the building. She wasn't ugly but those people were movie-star beautiful and lord, they were so young. She couldn't compete with them. She'd had three children. It showed.

She started the car and then turned it off. Damnit, Craig wasn't young either. A couple got out of their car. They were about her age, well dressed and attractive, but she could compete with people like them. Sure her body wasn't the tight, firm one of her younger years, but she still looked good. She had a slight curve to her stomach—something she couldn't get rid of no matter how much she exercised—and her breasts weren't exactly perky any more, but the push-up bra helped.

She glanced down and flushed. She was practically spilling out of the dress. She started to tug the neckline upward but stopped. There was no point in hiding her best asset. She was going to show Craig exactly what he'd thrown away with his infidelity.

CHAPTER 9: CRAIG

Craig sat at the bar in the Club, nursing his second drink. He'd been here over an hour and Liz still hadn't arrived. Perhaps, she'd come to her senses and realized what a stupid idea this was.

A woman walked over to him. "May I sit?"

He was flattered. She was an attractive brunette—younger than him, late thirties perhaps. She had long, long legs and great tits. Probably fake, because they were way too big for her frame, but they were nice.

"Ah..." He glanced at the door. He didn't need Liz seeing him with someone else.

"Are you waiting for someone in particular?"

"Yeah. Sorry." He smiled.

She shrugged. "Maybe another night?"

"Sure." He doubted it. Even if he ended up getting a divorce, he probably wouldn't hang out at the Club.

There were plenty of men his age and women too, but there were also so many kids. Many of them were working—both men and women. They were all uniquely attractive in some way but even though Ethan wouldn't hire anyone underage, they were still kids to him. He couldn't imagine having sex with someone the same age as one of his daughters.

"Another?" asked the bartender.

"Sure. Why not?" If Liz didn't show he may as well get drunk. He had nothing else to do on Christmas Eve.

"It's on me, and bring me one too," Ethan took the seat next to Craig.

"Thanks."

"She'll show," said Ethan.

"I'm not so sure."

The bartender returned with their drinks.

"To alcohol on Christmas." He raised his glass.

"The only thing that gets me through." Ethan raised his brandy snifter.

He laughed but it was sad and they both knew it.

"She'll show," repeated Ethan.

"Yeah." He still wasn't so sure about that but..."What if she recognizes me?" He really wanted to say, what if she turned him down. What if she picked one of these twenty-year-old guys and went into the back?

Ethan took a moment and studied him. "She won't. You look great."

"Gee, thanks." He felt like an idiot. Ethan had given him a dark green domino that covered his head and most of his face. Only his eyes and lips were actually visible. If that weren't bad enough, Ethan had added a hat. He never wore hats but tipped down at an angle, it did help hide his face.

"Remember, you're a sexy man." Ethan laughed as he pulled his phone from his pocket. He looked at it, sobering. "She's here."

"Where?" Craig scanned the crowd of well-dressed people in masks.

"Just came through the doors." Ethan stood, looking toward the front of the room. "She should be here any min...There she is."

All the blood rushed to Craig's dick. She looked fabulous. She wore a gold dress that hugged her curves and highlighted the gold in her hair. It was piled on top of her head in a loose knot of some sort that looked like one tug would cause it to tumble down around her body, cascading over her breasts which were displayed to perfection. The gown was very low cut, causing her creamy mounds to sway as she walked. He held his breath. They seemed destined to pop from the dress any moment.

More than one set of eyes followed her path. Craig struggled not to run to her and throw his jacket around her shoulders. Those breasts and that ass belonged to him. None one else was allowed to look.

"She's lovely," said Ethan. "I knew she was attractive but..."

"Shut the fuck up." She was his. His wife. No papers had been signed. No papers would be signed.

"Have fun and...uhm..."

"Yes?" He tore his eyes away from his wife.

"Don't be afraid to try something new. It might be exactly what you both need."

"We don't need kinky sex games."

"Are you sure? Apparently, you need something...different."

He tossed back his drink, refusing to comment. He didn't like it but the man was right. Something had gone wrong between them and he had no idea how to fix it.

"Go get her and...play, but don't let her know it's you."

"Right." He wasn't so sure about this. They'd been married a long time. He'd had no problem recognizing her even with the small, gold and black mask covering the top part of her face.

"Relax." Ethan waved the bartender over. "Have another drink and get to know your wife again." He slapped him on the shoulder. "I told the bouncers you have full access to the Club so try out a few of the rooms and enjoy."

The rooms? He couldn't take Liz there, could he? He glanced at his wife. She was sitting at the bar, looking a bit nervous. The bartender delivered her drink. She smiled and Craig's stomach clenched. He loved her smile. She paid the bartender and then took a sip of her margarita—her red lips wrapping around that straw and sucking. His dick was rock hard in an instant. It'd been a long time since he'd felt those lips on his cock. Too long. Tonight was going to end that drought.

CHAPTER 10: LIZ

Liz made her way to the bar and sat, trying not to gawk. This was not at all what she'd expected a sex club to look like. This place was extraordinary. There was a huge Christmas tree, fully decorated and there was garland and lights everywhere. It was beautiful and so were the people. She'd never been around this many attractive people in her life. She wanted to find a corner, grab a bowl of popcorn and watch them. They could be her new favorite television show.

A man dipped his head to kiss a woman as his hand crept under her skirt.

Okaaay. Make that her new favorite HBO show. The woman spread her legs and the man shifted, his hand obviously in places it shouldn't be...at least not in public. She turned away, blushing.

"What's your pleasure?" asked the bartender, smiling slightly. He had blonde hair and blue eyes. His shoulders were wide and hips slim. He was one of the hottest men she'd seen in her life.

"Ah...a margarita. Rocks. With salt."

"Got it." He winked and left.

She looked around. Craig was here somewhere. She had no idea what she'd do when she found him. Confront him? Leave with someone else? If anyone was interested in her. She closed her eyes. She'd die if Craig saw her and no one even tried to pick her up.

"Anything else?" The bartender put her drink down in front of her.

"Ah..." If she were going to flirt and maybe leave with a stranger she needed more than a margarita. "Yes. A shot of tequila, please."

"First time?" He asked.

"That obvious?" Great. She stood out like a beacon of insecurity.

"Nope, but I work a lot and I would've remembered you." His eyes dipped to her chest.

"Oh. Thank you." Her face heated. It'd been a long time since any man besides Craig had looked at her like that.

"Thank *you*." He grinned, his eyes roaming over her breasts in hot regard before leaving.

She almost fanned herself. If no one else appeared, the bartender would do nicely. All she had to do was find her husband so he could see the other man flirting with her. She picked up her drink and took a sip as she covertly searched the room. A man, sitting across the bar, was staring at her. A trickle of unease tickled her spine. There was a predatory look to his gaze that both scared her and made her squeeze her thighs together in anticipation. She was woman enough to know exactly what a look like that meant.

"Here you go." The bartender put a shot, a lime and a salt shaker in front of her.

"Thanks. May I start a tab?"

"Absolutely. I'll need to see your driver's license."

She dug in her purse and gave it to him.

He jotted down her name and handed it back. "Enjoy, Elizabeth."

"I plan on it." She glanced across the bar but the man who'd been looking at her was gone. She frowned as she tossed back the shot. It was probably for the best. He'd looked kind of angry and more than a little dangerous.

"May I join you?" A very attractive, young man stood by her side.

"Sure." She motioned to the chair.

"I'm Charlie." He sat and held out his hand.

"Hi, Charlie." She shook his hand, noticing the bracelet he wore. Oh God, he was a...prostitute. Of course, that's not what they called it and technically it wasn't how it worked. That had been made perfectly clear before she'd been allowed to enter.

She'd been informed of all the rules by the muscular bouncer who'd checked ids and invitations.

Rule number one: Consent for all things is a must. Rule two: Employees wore bracelets with the Club's insignia. And rule number three, the most important one: No one pays for sex. The clients leave a stipend with the manager for an employee's time. The bouncer had been very serious, but it was a joke. Everyone knew what was actually being bought and sold.

"I haven't see you here before? Did you just join or are you still considering your invitation?" Charlie's dark eyes sparkled behind his blue mask.

"Considering." Saying she'd been denied membership and was only here because of a mistake probably wasn't a good idea.

"You should join." He leaned closer, his eyes dipping to her cleavage. "You'll meet a lot of new friends."

"Ah...thanks." She fought not to cover her chest with her hands. "Would you like something to drink?" She was the one with money. This poor kid was trying to earn a living.

"I got it." He waved the bartender over. "Two shots and a rum and coke."

"Thanks...but aren't you...shouldn't I—"

He took her hand. His was warm and strong. "You're supposed to enjoy yourself." He kissed her fingers. "Let me help you."

"Ah...I don't. You're so young." She bit her lip. "Sorry. I didn't mean to say that out loud."

"I'm over eighteen and that's all that matters, right?"

He was drinking in the bar so he must be at least twenty-one, but that was only a little older than Robbie. She couldn't do this. Not with him. "I'm sorry. I can't." She lowered her voice. "You're my son's age."

He laughed. "We're only talking and"—he leaned by her ear—"I'm not your son. I'm a man who's very attracted to you." His hand brushed her knee.

God, he smelled good and he was warm. The heat radiated off him. Part of her wanted to snuggle up against him, but she couldn't. It'd be wrong. He may think he was a man but he was still a boy to her. She pulled away when the bartender brought their drinks.

"Cheers," said Charlie as he picked up his shot.

"Cheers." She lifted her glass, her eyes darting to his other drink. A rum and coke. That was what Craig drank. She loved the taste of it on his lips. Would it taste differently on Charlie's?

He tossed back his tequila and put the glass on the bar. "Your turn."

"Right." She swallowed the alcohol, grimacing as she bit into the lime.

"Another?" His dark eyes were studying her breasts.

"No. I'd better slow down." She was already warm and tingly and the night was still young. She hadn't even seen Craig yet.

"Why? I'll take care of you." His lips turned up in a wicked quirk. "I'll take very good care of you."

"The lady said no." A man sat down on her other side.

Charlie's eyes slowly moved up her body, until he was staring over her shoulder. She turned toward the other gentleman and her heart sped. It was the same man who'd been staring at her from across the bar.

"I was only asking," said Charlie.

"And she answered." The man spoke in low tones but his voice sent a tingle down her spine.

This was a man, not a boy. She couldn't make out his face because of the mask and his hat but she could tell by the lines around his mouth and the build of his body that he was well past his twenties, maybe even past thirty.

"Thank you, but Charlie wasn't going to force me to do anything I didn't want to do. Even something as simple as having another shot." She didn't desire Charlie but she didn't want this man thinking she needed him to take care of her.

"And what do you want?" The man glanced at her, his eyes dropping to her breasts for one quick second.

That was a good question. At first, she'd come to get even with Craig but there was something about this man that was making her body melt. "I want to enjoy myself."

"That can be arranged." He waved the bartender over. "A shot of tequila for me and..." He turned toward her.

"Why not?" It was Christmas Eve. She had no desire to go home alone.

"Excuse me." Charlie stood.

Great. Now, she'd pissed off the boy. Men his age got hurt so easily. She turned toward him, smiling. "It was lovely..."

He leaned by her ear. "Find me if you change your mind." He kissed her cheek and left.

Well, he took that better than she'd expected. Of course, she'd only been a job to him. She took a large gulp of her margarita. She hadn't wanted Charlie but she'd foolishly allowed herself to be flattered by his attention.

The bartender delivered their drinks and left.

"Here's to enjoying the evening." The man handed her a glass, his fingers sliding over hers.

She felt that touch inside her—deep inside. She stared at his hands. They were strong with long fingers—fingers that could give so much pleasure. She quickly tossed back the drink. What was she thinking? She didn't even know this man. She shouldn't be this attracted to him, but her body screamed—why not? He was a man and she was a woman who hadn't had sex in far too long. Ever since she'd found the membership card she hadn't been able to let Craig touch her.

He tossed back his drink. "Are you okay?"

"Yeah." She smiled but her lips trembled. No, she wasn't okay. She should be home watching a Christmas movie with her husband not flirting with a stranger.

"You sure? You don't look okay."

"I'm...I'm sorry." None of this was his fault.

"It's okay." He actually seemed relieved. "I understand. This place can be...something else."

"It's not that." She took a gulp of her margarita. "I...It's not important." She didn't need to burden him with her problems.

"Tell me." He turned toward her.

"I can't." She stared across the bar. "It's embarrassing and you don't want to hear about my problems."

"Sure I do."

"Why?" She glanced at him, her eyes going to his wrist. "You don't work here, do you?"

He laughed. "No. I'm...a member but I don't come here often."

"Why not?" She would've thought any man who could afford membership would practically live here.

"I'll tell you after you've told me what's wrong."

"It's nothing. I-I'm going through a divorce and—"

"What happened?"

"The usual. He cheated."

"He..." His body stiffened. He cleared his throat. "Are you sure?"

"I'm positive. I guess"—she took a fortify gulp of her drink—"I'm here because I want to get even with him for that."

"That's why you're doing this?" He stood, forcing a smile. "Excuse me. I need to use the rest room." His back was stiff as he walked away.

Apparently, he didn't like the idea of cheating husbands any more than she did. Her eyes dropped to his ass. It was firm and round in his black dress slacks. She wouldn't mind nibbling on that tush. Her gaze roamed up his frame—nice broad shoulders, a slender waist although not as slender as when he'd been younger. Her mouth dropped open. She knew that for a fact. That bastard.

She turned to the bartender. "Another round and make it a double." She was going to tear into him when he returned. How dare he pretend to be someone else.

The bartender put two doubles down on the bar and left. She grabbed one and drank it, relishing the burn. He was probably laughing at her right now. The warmth of the tequila filled her throat. Craig's eyes hadn't been laughing when he'd looked at her. They'd been dark and full of desire and...hurt. He'd gotten pissed when she'd said he'd cheated. Too bad, he was here, wasn't he? She grabbed his shot and tossed it back. Oh, he was going to pay for this. For all of it—the cheating, the pain, the pretending.

He came out of the bathroom and headed toward her. Her eyes raked over his body—so familiar, so loved. God help her, she wanted him. He was stopped by a young woman wearing a bracelet. Was that how it'd been? These young women—girls Tina and Ellie's age—hitting on him, making him feel young again. Well, tonight she was going to show him what he threw away. She wasn't some young girl. She was a woman and she was going to give him a night to remember—a night to make him forget every one of these girls and regret every indiscretion he'd ever made.

She waved the bartender over. "May I have a piece of paper?"

"Sure." He handed her a notepad and pen. He started to walk away.

"Hold on. This will only be a minute." She jotted a note for Craig and folded it. She glanced his way. He was walking toward her again. "Please put this with my...friend's bill."

"Okay." The bartender stared at the folded paper in his hands.

"It's a game we play."

"Oh." He smiled and walked away, obviously, quite used to weird games played by the clientele.

Craig sat down and picked up his drink. It was rum and coke. She should've known it was him. How had she not? She knew those hands, that body. His cologne was different but familiar too. It was a scent she'd given him a few years ago but he hadn't worn. She was going to kill him.

"I was thinking." She touched his arm.

"Yeah." He turned toward her, his eyes still hurt and angry.

"Maybe, you could help me get even with my cheating husband." The muscle in his jaw twitched when she said cheating and she struggled not to grin.

"I could do that, but are you sure?"

"Absolutely. He cheated on me. I deserve some fun too."

"Are you positive he cheated? I mean, how do you know? Why do you think that?"

"What are you, his lawyer?"

"No. It's just..." He stared hard into her eyes. "My wife accused me of cheating but she was wrong. If she'd talked to me—"

"I did. He lied." Oh, she was so close to ending this farce. "I found his membership to this Club."

"That...that can...could be explained."

She'd caught him off guard. Good. "I doubt it, but it doesn't matter. I saw him."

"That's impossible." He cleared his throat again.

"My *husband* wishes it were."

"No. I mean, really, you couldn't have seen him."

She was done. She stood. "I didn't come to talk about my soon to be ex. I came here to...get fucked." She'd go find Charlie. God, no, that wouldn't work. He was too young but she'd find someone else.

CHAPTER 11: CRAIG

"No." Craig grabbed Liz's arm. He had no idea what she thought she'd seen, but she didn't see him cheat. She should've talked to him about it, but obviously that wasn't going to happen. At least not until after they fucked because he was going to have her tonight.

"No?" She jerked free from his grip. "You don't get to tell me no."

He took a deep steadying breath. Anger never worked with Liz. "I think we can help each other." He rested his hand on her arm, running his thumb over her soft skin.

"How? You seem more interested in talking than doing. My husband wasn't interested in my body either and—"

"That's not true!" He'd lain awake too many nights, hard and ready but afraid to wake her because he knew she'd refuse him.

"You say that like you know." She studied him, a slight smirk on her lush, red lips.

"I do." He had to control his mouth because he was not losing this one opportunity to fix things between them.

"Really?" Her brow raised in challenge.

"Yeah, because he'd have to be a blind fool not to want you." His eyes locked with hers and then traveled downward, stopping on her lips before moving to her breasts.

"Oh. Thank you." Her hand came up, blocking his view.

"Don't thank me yet." He took her hand, caressing her wrist with his thumb and feeling the pulse increase with his attentions. "Please, sit." He forced himself to drop his hold. She had to make this choice herself. She had to choose him.

She didn't say anything but she took the seat next to him.

"Another round." He waved to the bartender.

"When should I thank you?" She glanced at him out of the corner of her eyes.

"Later." He took one of the shots from the bartender and handed it to her. "After we've gotten to know each other better." He smiled as he picked up his tequila. "To a night of pleasure." He held up his glass and tossed back the liquor.

"To a night of pleasure." She did the same. "So, what should we do first?"

He wanted to say—first, I'm going to take you home and...what? Fuck her? Punish her? Both were very appealing but he had no idea what she wanted. He hadn't in a long time. He needed to change that. "What's something you wanted to do with your husband but never did?"

She gave him an odd look.

Perhaps, he shouldn't mention her husband. "I'm asking because there are things I would've liked to have done. My wife..."

"Your wife what?" There was ice in her tone.

Good. It served her right for even thinking about having sex with a stranger. "My wife deserves to be punished."

"For what?" She clamped her mouth shut. "I mean, what did she do? In my experience, it's the husband who—"

"I know you believe your husband cheated."

"He did." She almost snarled.

"This isn't getting us anywhere." *Except closer to a divorce.*

"No. It's not." She crossed her arms over her chest and his eyes almost popped from his head as those luscious mounds pushed upward, threatening to spill out.

"Let's go someone more private." He stood and offered her his hand. He wanted to get her out of that dress and onto his dick.

"I'm not ready to go to a private room with you."

Damn. He was more than ready. "Then let's go to one of the couches."

This room had a spattering of couches, lounge chairs, raised platforms and tables all around. She took his hand and he led her to one of the lesser occupied areas. He sat next to her on the couch, his leg pressed against hers.

"So, now what?" She was watching him closely.

"Now, I suggest we stop talking about our exes."

"I have a better suggestion." She waved a waitress over. "Another drink for each of us."

"Shot?" he asked.

"Why not?" She smiled and his heart lurched. This was the girl he'd married—bold, flirtatious and adventurous.

"Two more tequilas, a margarita and a rum and coke," he said to the waitress.

When she left he shifted so he was facing Liz. She was leaning against the back of the couch but didn't look comfortable. Her skirt was short and she kept trying to keep it at a decent level.

He placed his hand on her knee. "Let me help you." He put his other hand on the other side of her hip, blocking her body from the room. "Now, you don't have to worry about your dress." Her skin was so soft that he couldn't keep from caressing her leg, letting his hand skim upward a little more.

"What are you doing?" She grabbed his wrist, but the part of her face he could see under her mask was flushed and her eyes were dark with desire.

He moved his fingers, stroking along her inner thigh. "A night of pleasure, remember?" He bent his head and kissed her neck where it met her shoulder. "Let me give you that."

"Here? Everyone can see us." There was a breathless, excited quality to her voice.

"No one is watching. No one cares." He kissed her neck again. God, she tasted so good. His lips moved downward toward her breasts.

CHAPTER 12: LIZ

Liz's fingers loosened on Craig's hand as his lips moved down her neck. She couldn't do this. They couldn't do this. What had gotten into him? Is this what he did with those other women? "Stop." She pushed at his head, wishing he'd take off the stupid hat and mask. "The waitress."

The waitress put the drinks down as unobtrusively as she could. Craig sat up and handed her some cash. "I have a tab. This is for you."

"Thanks." The waitress smiled and walked away, seeming not at all bothered by what she'd witnessed.

Craig handed Liz a shot and she tossed it back. She'd need it if she were going to push him to his limits because his limits were more than she'd imagined.

He picked up his glass and stared at it a moment before setting it down. "I need salt." He shifted in front of her again and lowered his face. His hot mouth grazed the top of her breast, his tongue slipping under her dress. She gasped, her hands grasping his shoulders. She'd missed this so much. Too much.

He moaned against her chest and his kiss became rougher. His fingers dipped inside her gown and he popped her breast from the cloth.

"Cr...Wait."

But he didn't listen. His mouth was on her nipple, sucking and teasing. She forgot why she was protesting, forgot everything but that mouth and those feelings surging through her body. Her hands clutched at his head, knocking off his hat. She needed to tangle her fingers in his thick, soft hair. She started to push the mask away.

He grabbed her wrist as he lifted his lips a fraction. "Rules." His hot breath caressed her skin. "We can't take off our masks unless we go to a private room."

"Fine." Her hands dropped to his shoulders, pulling him toward her.

He smiled against her breast and licked her nipple. She wiggled underneath him. She needed more than that.

"What do you want?" he asked against her skin.

She grabbed his head again, angling him toward her nipple.

"Tell me."

She was not going to say it.

"Beg me, Liz."

"How do you know my name?" She wanted to cram the words back into her mouth. If he revealed who he was, she'd have to leave and she didn't want to leave. She wanted to be with him, just one more time—feel him hard and heavy inside her, around her.

His face was frozen against her chest and then he smiled. "I heard you tell that kid at the bar."

"Oh. Right." She was impressed with his lie, although she shouldn't be. He'd been lying to her for years.

He kissed his way toward her nipple.

"Wait."

He sighed, his warm breath teasing her sensitive skin as he tore his gaze away from her chest. "Yes?"

"What's your name?" Since he didn't want to end this charade either, she might as well push him.

"Ah...Chris. My name's Chris."

"It's nice to meet you...Chris." For guy who made a fortune in advertising, her husband wasn't very creative. Christopher was his middle name.

"You too, Liz." His eyes dropped back to her breast. "Now, where were we." He ran his tongue over her nipple. It was hot and wet, but too soft and fleeting. He did it again, this time flicking her little bud and sending streaks of desire shooting straight between her legs.

People began moving toward them. He kissed all around her nipple, teasing her. She tried to focus on him, the feelings he was stirring inside her, but people were gathering around them.

"Stop. They're watching." She shoved at him and he sat up, blocking her bared breast with his body.

She pulled her dress up.

"They're not watching us." He was looking over his shoulder.

She leaned to the side, staring around him. A few feet away on a stage, a woman was bent over a small wooden stand. Her hands and legs were cuffed to the base and she was naked. A man stood behind her, wearing jeans and a black mask, his chest bare—and ripped. She touched her mouth to make sure she wasn't drooling.

The man had black hair, a strong jaw and a face that could cause a nun to sin. He had a slight five-o'clock shadow and the sexiest lips she'd ever seen. "Jesus."

"He's not that attractive." Craig shot her a dirty look.

She couldn't help it, she laughed. "Yes, he is." Let him feel jealous for a moment.

"Let's go." He took her hand.

"No. I want to watch." Mainly, to annoy him but also, because she wanted to see what was going to happen. The man circled the woman, his hand drifting down her back to her ass. "Can you hear what he's saying?" The murmurs of the crowd covered his words.

"No." Craig shifted so he could see the stage without craning his neck, but he kept the length of his body pressed against hers.

"What's he going to do to her?"

"What do you think." It wasn't a question.

The man on stage already had a huge bulge pressing against his jeans. She couldn't look away. She'd never seen anyone have sex before except in the pornos she and Craig had watched early in their marriage. It'd led to fantastic sex. She had no idea why they'd stopped. Oh yeah, the kids.

The man looked over the crowd and someone handed him a small flayed whip.

"He's going to hit her?" She grabbed Craig's hand. They'd never watched anything like this.

"Looks like it." His voice was rough.

Did he want to do that? "Have you ever..."

He looked at her. "No."

His green eyes were so familiar—the heat, the desire. Things she hadn't seen in them for too long. She leaned toward him, unable not to. His eyes dropped to her mouth and she licked her lips. The sharp scream of pain that turned into a moan of pleasure broke her trance. Her head snapped toward the stage. The man hit the woman again. The lady moaned, low and throaty, but she didn't scream this time.

"I...She likes it." More wetness pooled between her legs.

"Yeah." His hand tightened around hers.

She swallowed. What would it feel like to be hit? She'd never imagined that it'd be enjoyable but this woman seemed to like it. A lot.

The man whipped her again before massaging her ass to sooth the sting. He dropped to his knees and kissed up her thighs. The woman moaned, long and low. Liz squeezed her legs together. Her panties were soaked.

Craig leaned closer. "This is turning you on, isn't it?"

"No."

"Liar." His lips brushed the shell of her ear, causing her to shiver.

"Like you aren't?" Her gaze dropped to the bulge in his pants. She wasn't the only one getting into this.

"I was hard for you before this started." His hand moved to her leg. "Were you wet for me? Before this."

She wasn't going to answer that.

"Should I find out for myself?" His hand moved between her thighs, pushing the dress with it.

"We can't." She grasped his wrist but didn't actually try to stop him. "There are too many people around."

"No one is watching us." He kissed her neck. "Relax and watch the show." He captured her chin, his lips catching hers for a quick second before turning her face toward the stage.

The man had his face buried in the woman's pussy and she was writhing against her restraints.

Craig's hands moved upward—his fingers long and rough against the sensitive skin of her inner thigh. The man on stage spread the woman's legs wider, letting everyone see how wet she was.

"Open for me." Craig's voice was a hot whisper in her ear.

Without thinking, her legs fell apart and his fingers were there, right where she needed them. She bit her lip, trying to stop her moan—the pressure of his touch almost enough to send her spiraling into orgasm. She took a deep, shaky breath. She didn't want to come too soon. She wanted this to last.

"You're so fucking hot." He said in her ear as he pushed aside her underwear. "And wet. Are you wet for me or for him?" His finger slid between her folds and she shifted her hips, giving him better access. "Tell me." He nipped her neck, pulling his hand back a fraction.

She grabbed his wrist, holding him to her. He couldn't stop, not now. "Please," she whispered.

"Answer me." He slid a finger inside of her and her body bucked, pleading for more.

"Please." She needed him to move his hand. She needed friction, lovely hot, hard friction.

"Me or him." He was stroking inside her now, his finger and voice hard and tense.

She bit her lip, refusing to admit that he'd done this to her. He didn't deserve to know.

"Tell me, or I stop." He stroked faster his thumb teasing her clit.

The woman on stage cried out with release and the man stood. He wiped his mouth on his arm and undid his pants.

"Oh my God." That man was huge.

Craig shoved three fingers inside her as his thumb pressed down on her clitoris.

It was all she needed. All she could handle. Her body tightened and she cried out, her hips thrusting against his hand as she came.

CHAPTER 13: CRAIG

"That was wonderful...Chris." Liz's eyes were almost closed and there was a slight smile on her gorgeous lips. The lips that'd called him another man's name.

"You weren't supposed to come." Craig wanted to kiss her, throttle her and fuck her until she screamed his name.

"I'd say sorry"—she grinned—"but I'm not."

She was sexy as fuck and he couldn't stay mad at her, not with her chest flushed from the passion he'd given her. "Come here."

She swatted at his hand. "No, you stay right there and watch the show." She captured his jaw, turning him toward the stage, like he'd done to her.

The guy, who had the biggest dick he'd ever seen, was positioned behind the woman. He was about to see live porn. He was going to come in his pants. Liz's small hand skimmed over his erection.

He caught her wrist. "Don't start this unless you're planning on finishing it." He was in no mood to be teased.

"Oh, I'm going to finish this." She kissed his ear and he moaned. "Even you deserve a happy ending sometimes."

Her hand slid inside his pants. He sighed as he relaxed against the couch.

"Don't watch me. Watch them. Like everyone else." She gave his dick a firm squeeze.

"I'd rather watch you." He turned so his lips were a hair's breadth from hers.

"Then, I stop." She removed her hand from his pants.

"I'll watch." He had no choice. His body, too long starved for her touch, would revolt if he let this opportunity pass.

The man with the giant cock was sliding inside the woman, inch by agonizing inch. Liz unzipped his pants and he lifted so she could pull them down, freeing his aching erection.

The woman on stage was squirming, thrusting her ass toward the man, wanting more. He understood that completely. His hips rocked upward shoving his dick against her hand. She kissed his neck and grasped his cock, stroking up and down.

"Fuck, Liz. That feels so good."

The guy was rocking into the woman now and he found himself following his tempo. He wanted to be inside Liz like the guy was inside that woman, feeling her heat wrapped around him, her body clenching onto his, not wanting him to leave. Liz shifted again, moving away from his neck.

"Where are you going?" He didn't want her to move at all—except her hand. That had to keep moving.

"I promise, you won't be disappointed." She bent.

She was going to give him a blow job. She hadn't done that in a long time. His breath was tight as he waited. His dick twitching in anticipation.

She looked up at him, her mouth inches from his dick. "Don't watch me."

"That's impossible." He wanted to see her wrap those lips around his cock. He wanted to see his dick disappear between her hot, wet lips.

"Watch the stage." She licked his tip.

"Liz..." He closed his eyes, a guttural moan vibrating in his chest.

"Watch that man have sex with that woman...or I stop."

Her breath was hot on his dick but he needed her lips and tongue and mouth. God, he needed her mouth. He opened his eyes.

The guy had the woman's hips in his hands and was pounding into her. Her tits were jiggling from the force of his thrusts and her head was tipped, face filled with pleasure. Liz's mouth came down around his dick and he groaned. It felt too good, the wetness, the pressure. He shifted upward and she gagged but kept sucking. Her hand stroking his shaft as her mouth worked the top. All the while, the man fucked the woman. Their groans and the sounds of flesh against flesh, along with Liz's sucking was too much. His hips rocked, out of control. He bit down on his hand, the scent of her on his fingers filling his head. "Liz, baby. I'm gonna come." His hand wrapped in her hair, trying to pull her away but she grabbed his thighs and sucked harder. "Shit...I can't."

His balls tightened and he pushed her downward as he thrust up, her throat closing around him. He grunted as he came, his dick twitching with release. He expected her to pull away, but she kept sucking. His head dropped against the couch as he spurted into her again and again.

She lifted her head, his dick sliding from her mouth. He stroked her hair as he watched her through half-closed eyes. He'd never asked her to swallow before. He'd assumed she'd be disgusted. Perhaps, he didn't know his wife as well as he'd thought.

CHAPTER 14: LIZ

Liz couldn't believe she'd given Craig a blow job in public. A few people had glanced their way for a second but other than that no one cared.

"That was fantastic." He lifted his hips, stuffing that wonderful cock back into his pants and zipping up. He pulled her into his arms, kissing her softly. "Thank you."

Her emotions warred. She wanted to relax against him, but she couldn't. He'd cheated on her, before and again, just now. He didn't know who she was and he'd let her suck his cock. She pulled away from him and stood, flagging down a waitress. "I'm sure you've had better."

"What? No. I've never done that before."

"A blow job? Please. I know better." They used to do oral a lot, but somehow it'd gotten lost along the way just like his love for her.

The waitress walked over.

"A water and a shot of tequila." She looked down at him. His green eyes were confused and a little sad. An ache flared in her chest where her heart had been before he'd destroyed it. "Do you want anything or are you done for the night?"

His face hardened. "A shot of tequila."

"Got it." The waitress left.

"Come here." He grabbed her hand, tugging her toward him. "We need to talk."

"That's the last thing we need to do." She pulled free from his grasp. If they did that this was over.

A scream of release caught their attention. The woman on stage looked almost boneless, her body hanging across the wooden stand. The man thrust into her again and then stiffened, his body jerking with his release. He stepped back, pulling up his pants before bending and unhooking her. He wrapped her in his arms and carried her off the stage. A knot formed in Liz's throat at his tenderness. She wiped at her eyes. She was not going to cry over a sex scene even if it reminded her of how Craig had been during her first pregnancy. He hadn't been able to do enough for her. By the third child, he was working late hours, trying to get the business off the ground. Had he been lying even then? Fucking some other woman while she'd been heavy with his child?

"Liz." He stood next to her. "Please. Come home with me and let's talk."

So, he'd recognized her. It didn't matter. If she admitted that she knew him, this would all end and she wanted one more night with him. She shook her head. "I don't know you."

"You know me well enough to suck my dick." He almost growled.

"Doesn't mean I'm going home with you."

His face was stone except for one muscle that twitched in his jaw. She'd never seen him so furious.

"Fine. You want to stay. I got an idea."

"What?"

The waitress brought their drinks. Liz took a swallow of her water, washing down the taste of him.

"Since we both seem to have latent issues with our exes—"

"Apparently." She picked up her shot.

"I suggest that we pretend the other is our ex and take out all our hostility on them."

She froze, glass near her mouth. "I don't want to fight with you." It may have been her plan in the beginning but now that she was here and a little drunk, she wanted sex. With him. One last time, so he'd know exactly what he'd thrown away.

He grinned and electricity zinged to her toes. "I'm not talking about fighting. I'm talking about fucking." He moved closer and she could feel how much stronger and bigger he was than her. "I'm talking about doing all those things—those secret things—we wanted to do but were afraid to suggest."

"Is that why you cheated?" She'd had no idea he'd wanted more than what they'd done. Sure their sex life had gotten a little predictable but she'd always enjoyed it.

"I didn't cheat," he said through clenched teeth. "My wife left me. For no good reason and I'm a little pissed about that." He tossed back his shot. "Are you in?"

CHAPTER 15: LIZ

"For no good reason?" Liz struggled not to slap his handsome face. "She had...I'm sure she had plenty of good reasons."

"I'd love to hear them."

She opened her mouth and clamped it shut. She wasn't done with tonight, with him. It was Christmas Eve. She deserved a present and a night of sex with her soon to be ex-husband was just what Santa ordered.

She'd been hot for him since the moment they'd met. He'd arrived late to class and had sat by her. He'd smelled like shampoo and male. She'd been so flustered and shy she'd barely spoken to him.

"Like I figured. You can't think of one reason my wife would leave me." He towered over her, his anger barely restrained.

She wanted to push him until he lost control, until he felt a little of the hurricane of hurt and anger that surged through her. "Are we going to talk or take out our frustrations." She stepped closer, her breasts brushing against his chest. "I have to warn you. I'm more than frustrated with my husband. I'm furious."

"That's perfect. I feel the same about my wife." He almost spat the last word.

"Then how do we do this?"

"We both want the truth, right?" His eyes gleamed.

"Yes." She knew he'd cheated but she wanted to hear him say it. It was the only way she'd ever be able to get over him.

"Let's make a wager. We'll take turns suggesting...activities and if the other person refuses, she—"

"Or he," she corrected.

"Or he, must answer one question. Honestly. Completely honestly."

"So, if I suggest you have sex with a man and you refuse, you'll have to answer my question?"

"Wait a minute."

She grinned. She'd have her questions answered in no time.

"We need some ground rules."

"I don't see why?"

"Great. You're willing to eat pussy. I'd love to watch that."

"I'm sure you would." Men were disgusting. "Okay. We can only suggest activities where both of us participate."

"And only us."

"You don't want a threesome?" She tried to be nonchalant but it hurt that he wanted other women, even if she were involved.

"No," he almost growled. "I just want you."

She fought it but a piece of her heart was resurrected. She couldn't allow that. It'd hurt too much when it died again. "For tonight only."

His jaw tightened as if he were fighting not to speak but eventually, he said, "Fine."

She could do this. She could let herself have sex with him tonight and then it was over. "Who goes first?'

"Ladies first."

"Okay." She bit her lip. She'd make him beg. Make him weep when he thought about everything he'd lost because he couldn't keep his dick in his pants. The problem was, she had no idea what to suggest. She'd been happy with their sex life. She glanced around for inspiration. The crowd had dispersed. The man who'd been on stage was sitting on a couch with the woman on his lap, offering her a drink and kissing her gently. That's what she wanted. That tenderness, that love, but she'd never admit that.

"Tick-tock. We don't have all night."

"Stop being an ass."

"I'd like to spank *your* ass."

"Okay." Her face heated and she was suddenly glad for the mask because it wasn't all from embarrassment.

"Really?" His eyes widened.

"Yes. I'll let you spank me." She loved surprising him and by the look on his face, this was a good one.

"Come on." His voice was rough with passion as he took her hand.

"No." She refused to move.

"But you said—"

"Not in some room hidden away." She pointed at the stage. "Up there." She shot him a challenging look. "Unless you're afraid you'll get stage fright." She let her eyes slide down his body to his crotch.

"I'm not afraid of anything." He yanked on her hand, pulling her against him.

Her nipples hardened as they rubbed against his chest. She wanted to scream. She hated that she still wanted him this much.

"Are you sure, Liz? Do you truly want me lifting your dress and spanking your ass in front of everyone? Trust me, this time they will watch."

Her heart raced. Did she want that? Could she do that?

"Or, are you ready to answer a question?"

"It was my idea." She shouldn't be punished for having a big mouth. She was drunk.

"Too bad. The offer was made. You refuse. You answer a question."

"I need another shot."

"Good old liquid courage." He waved the waitress over and ordered a double shot of tequila. He whispered in Liz's ear, "Is the thought of being up there, tied to the post, your ass on display making you wet?"

"You're a dick." Heat rushed through her body. He'd never spoken to her like that.

When they'd first started dating they'd been so young that it'd been all love and kisses. Then the kids had come and sex had become something quick they did when the kids were sleeping, if they weren't too exhausted. Later, once the kids were older, they'd never found the time to experiment.

He gave the waitress a tip and handed Liz the shot. "Drink up. My hand is itching."

She tossed back the tequila. Perhaps, that was why he'd strayed. Maybe, he'd wanted to do other things and had been afraid to suggest it. She'd show him that he should've said something because she was up for almost anything, even being punished while on display in front of a room full of strangers. *Oh God, please let them all be strangers.* She grabbed her margarita. The ice had melted but she needed whatever alcohol she could find. She chugged until it was empty and then put it on the table. "Let's go." She shoved away from him and strode to the stage.

CHAPTER 16: CRAIG

Craig's eyes were on his wife's ass as she walked away. There was no way she was going to go through with this.

She stopped at the stairs, looking at him over her shoulder. "Are you coming or should I get someone else?"

"Don't you dare." He hurried after her onto the stage.

The people in the area began to move closer, ready for the show.

Liz bent over the post, ass up. "Ready?" Her eyes sparkled with challenge.

"More than ready." He was hard again. He hadn't recovered like that since his twenties but the sight of his wife bent over, waiting for him to spank her turned him on like nothing had in years. However, his desire was tainted by hurt and anger. He was pretty sure she knew it was him, but what if she didn't or what if he hadn't been here? Would she be playing out these fantasies with someone else?

"We are doing this tonight, right?" she taunted.

There were a few chuckles from the gathering crowd.

"Yes. Right now." He strode across the stage and bent over her, his body resting along hers. He grabbed her wrist and fastened the Velcro around it, strapping her to one side of the post. "I'm going to spank that ass and make you sorry you left me."

"You?" She turned her head so her lips were a whisper away from his face. "Don't you mean my husband? We're pretending, remember?"

"Yeah. Right." That confirmed it. She knew it was him. His dick hardened even more as he hooked her other hand and started to lift off her.

"Don't hit me too hard. Please." She glanced at him and there was fear in her eyes.

"Are you sure about this?" He grabbed her chin.

"I'm not losing. I'm not answering your question."

He almost said to hell with the question but he needed to know why she was so sure he'd cheated on her. Why she was willing to throw everything away on a hunch. "Then, I'm going to spank you until you come."

"That will never happen." She turned her face away, a stubborn tilt to her chin that he knew too well.

"We'll see about that." He straightened and moved behind her. God, she was hot—her ass in the air, waiting on him. She couldn't run away, not now. She was his. He ran his hands over her butt, squeezing. She didn't move but her breathing was as unsteady as his.

"Don't forget to tie her legs," shouted someone.

He glanced over his shoulder. The crowd wasn't as big as for the last show but there were quite a few people gathered around the stage. "You sure about this, Liz?"

"Are you ready to lose the bet?"

"Nope." He bent, grabbing her foot and yanking it to the side. She gasped as he hooked another strap around her ankle. He leaned around her, his face so close to her ass that he couldn't resist a quick nip.

"Hey," she squeaked.

"That was nothing. You better tell me now if you've changed your mind." He prayed she didn't back down. He'd never imagined doing this but now that they were here, he wanted to see this through.

"Ask me again and you forfeit."

"Fair enough." He grabbed her other leg, pulling it to the strap on the other side, and locking it in place. He stood and his dick almost popped through his zipper.

She was bent over the post, her legs spread wide, waiting for him. Her dress had ridden up, due to the position of her legs and her panties were partially exposed. He wanted to shove her clothes out of the way and fuck her—hard—but that wasn't the deal. He took a deep breath to get his body under control and bent over her. "Ready to put on a show?"

"Just get on with it."

"Whatever you want, darling." His hand came down hard on her ass and she squeaked. He straightened. "You need to be punished."

"So, you think."

"That's no way to talk to the man you belong to." She was his in every sense. She was his wife. His lover. His partner. His. He hit her again, the crack echoing in the room.

"I'm not yours. Not anymore."

"That smart mouth is going to get you in trouble." He skimmed his hand down her spine and over her butt, relishing the soft firmness, before slapping it again.

She whimpered and the sound was like a punch to his gut.

"I'll let you off easy...if you apologize."

"For what?" She tipped her head, trying to see him but couldn't with the restraints keeping her in place.

"Where should I start, Liz?" He'd laugh if it didn't hurt so much.

"Why don't you start by apologizing to me?"

"That's it." He was sick of her accusing him of cheating. He shoved her dress up and his breath caught in his chest. She was wearing a thong, her smooth, round ass bare for him. He glanced around—all those hungry eyes staring at his wife. He started to block their view, but she wanted this. She wanted all these men to see her—to see what belonged to him. His hand came down on her butt cheek and she squeaked again.

There was a red mark on her skin. It was his mark. He slapped the other cheek and she jumped. He moved closer, unable to stay away from her. He rested his hands on her angry flesh, massaging. "Are you ready to apologize?"

"No." She said through gritted teeth.

"You always were stubborn."

"Like you can talk."

There were a few snickers from the crowd but he ignored them. This was between him and her.

He slapped her ass again and grabbed her hips before bending and letting his tongue sooth the sting from his slaps. She stiffened, a soft moan slipping from her lips. He nipped her and she gasped. He kissed his way up her spine, shoving the dress out of his way. He'd love to tear it off and suck her tits but he wasn't going to put any more of her on display. She was his.

"Apologize." He straightened, letting his fingers trail up her thighs. "No."

He grasped her legs, shoving them farther apart. Her breath hitched and her body tensed, waiting for him. If they weren't on stage he'd be inside her right now. His thumbs drew little circles on the velvety softness of her inner thigh. "Are you wet?"

"Yes." Her voice was raw with desire.

His finger skimmed over the front of her panties. "You're soaked." He leaned down by her ear. "You like this, don't you? You want me to fuck you, don't you?"

"No."

"Your body is telling a different story." He stroked her pussy and she moaned.

"My body is lying. I hate you."

"But you want this." He shoved her panties aside and slid his finger into her.

"Oh god," she gasped.

He pushed another finger inside her. "Now, apologize."

"No." She was panting and wiggling her hips.

He curled his fingers, finding her g-spot.

"Oh, oh..." She tugged on her arms but couldn't move.

"Apologize."

She shook her head. "You first."

"I have nothing to apologize for." He slapped her ass as he stroked inward and she moaned long and loud. "Admit that you want this." He was past wanting her to apologize. Now, he needed her to admit that she wanted him—her husband.

"Please, Cr...please."

"Please who? Say my name." He stroked her faster, slapping her ass again and again. "Say it. Say my name."

"Chris. Please, Chris." She panted, emphasizing his name—that name.

"Fuck you, Liz." He jerked his fingers from her and she cried out. He wanted nothing more than to drop his pants and fuck her, but he couldn't. Not unless she admitted she knew it was him. He slapped her ass again. She did know it was him, didn't she?

"Please." Her body shook with unfulfilled need.

"Please what?" He leaned over her, letting his chest rest against her back and his dick on her ass. "What do you want, Liz? Tell me."

"Please, make me come." She wiggled her butt against his erection.

He moaned in her ear, rocking his hips into her for one glorious second before he shifted away. This wasn't over and if he kept rubbing on her it would be. "Who?" He slapped her thigh. "Who do you want to make you come?"

"You." It was barely a whisper.

"And who am I?" He nibbled her earlobe.

She took a deep breath. "A cheating bastard who's pretending to be my husband."

"Fuck this. I'm done." He shoved off her and walked to the other side of the stage. Maybe, she didn't know it was him. Maybe, his wife actually wanted a stranger to beat her.

"Coward," she yelled as the crowd parted.

Ethan and two bouncers made their way onto the stage. The bouncers moved to the side as Ethan bent in front of Liz, talking to her.

Craig tried but he couldn't make out one word that was being said. If she claimed she didn't want to do this he'd...He'd what? He wasn't going to hit her to hurt her. No matter how angry he was, he'd never do that. He could leave but his heart wouldn't let him do that either.

Ethan nodded and straightened, walking over to Craig.

"What?" He had no idea what Ethan was doing on stage.

"I'm glad you stopped."

"Why? Isn't this what your Club is about?" He'd done a lot less than the other guy who'd been on stage.

"No. Not at all." Ethan's eyes darkened. "The Club is about pleasure. Mutual pleasure." He turned and looked at Liz. "That was not what was going on here."

Ethan was right. It hadn't been about pleasure for either of them.

"Do you need to leave?" asked Ethan.

"You tell me. You're the boss." He was ready to go but only if Liz left with him.

Ethan grabbed his arm and pulled him to the side. "Can you handle this? I thought you could, but maybe I was wrong."

If he couldn't, the night was over. His marriage was over.

"Get it under control." Ethan's voice was a harsh whisper. "Don't let anger ruin this"—he glanced at Liz—"new phase in your relationship."

He stared at his wife, strapped down and vulnerable. Was that was this was? A new phase. A new chapter in their lives. They'd had young love and kids, work and home. Could they find each other again—Craig and Liz the couple?

"Everything is over if there's no pleasure." Ethan grabbed his chin. "Got it. It's all about pleasure. If there's no pleasure, there's no point."

If he and Liz couldn't find a way past the anger back to pleasure there'd be no love, no commitment, nothing. He nodded.

"You sure?" asked Ethan.

"Yeah." He had to do this. He loved her too much to lose her.

"Good," said Ethan. "I need you to trust me. Okay?"

"Why?" He didn't have a good feeling about this.

"I'm going to help you. That's all."

"How?"

Ethan's eyes went over his shoulder and before Craig knew what was happening the two bouncers had his arms.

"What the hell?" He struggled but there was no way he was moving.

"Trust me." Ethan turned and walked over to Liz.

CHAPTER 17: LIZ

Liz hung over the wooden stand, trying to hear what was going on behind her. Ethan and Craig were talking in whispers. What could they be discussing at a time like this? She tugged on her arms but she wasn't going anywhere, unless she asked. They would unhook her if she asked, right? Shit, shit, shit. How had she gotten herself into this? It'd been fine with only Craig up here, but Ethan...

She'd almost screamed when the man had appeared in front of her. She'd been so startled, she hadn't even considered how embarrassing this was. He'd asked if she were okay and she'd said yes, so why was he talking to Craig?

There were footsteps on the stage—big, heavy footsteps. Craig wouldn't let anyone else touch her, would he? She didn't want anyone but Craig. She blinked back tears. It wasn't fair. He'd been touching plenty of other women. Why couldn't she want Ethan?

A hand landed on her back, her bare back where Craig had raised her skirt. It was Craig's hand. It had to be. She looked between her legs. Those were not Craig's shoes.

"Your partner needs some lessons," Ethan said near her ear, his cologne fresh and enticing. "Shall I take over for him? Show him how to give a woman pleasure from pain?" His hand skimmed down her back and toward her ass.

"No. Stop." She didn't want his hand. She didn't want him.

"Stop?" Ethan's hand still, but he left it resting at the base of her spine. "Are you sure? I guarantee you'll enjoy everything I do to you." His voice was rich and deep, decadent with promises.

"No. Not you," she whispered, not wanting to admit her desire for her husband out loud.

"Not me." There was a hint of laughter in his tone. "I'm hurt."

"Sorry." She should let him touch her. Let Craig experience a little of the pain and jealousy he'd made her feel.

Ethan leaned over her, his lips by her ear. "Who do you want, Elizabeth?"

"Get off her," shouted Craig, but Ethan didn't move.

"My hus...him. Chris." That was the most she'd admit.

Ethan straightened and walked around her. He squatted, lifting her head so she stared into his blue eyes. "Does he know you know?" His voice was a whisper.

"I...I think so."

"What are you saying to her?" It was Craig and he wasn't happy.

"Go easy on him." Ethan touched her cheek, his finger caressing. "He never visited here for pleasure. He only came to talk to me about my business."

"Really?" She didn't know why she believed him. Men lied for each other all the time, but there was something honest and honorable about him—or maybe, she just wanted to believe his lies.

"Yes." His eyes searched hers and then he straightened. "Let him go."

In a second Craig was behind her, pulling her dress down and covering her ass.

"No. Don't." She didn't want to stop. She didn't want to face Craig or reality. She wanted to stay here being desired by her husband.

CHAPTER 18: CRAIG

Craig stepped away from Liz, her words like a slap. She didn't want him to touch her.

"You want to continue this scene?" Ethan's eyes sparkled with amusement.

"Yes...but not with you."

"With who then, Elizabeth?" asked Ethan.

"I already said."

She had? When? Craig hadn't been able to hear anything but their whispers.

"He needs to hear it, Elizabeth," said Ethan. "Who do you want to punish you? To fuck you."

"Chris. The man who was"—her face below her mask flushed with color—"spanking me."

Those words were like rain to a parched earth. It was all he needed. She wanted him, at least for right now, and he could turn right now into forever.

"She's all yours." Ethan handed him a key. "For later." He walked away, the bouncers following.

Craig stared at her for a moment, not sure where to start. He wanted to carry her to a room where he could make love to her, but she wanted this scene. His Liz wanted to be spanked—by him. His dick pressed against his zipper. He placed his hand on her thigh, enjoying the satiny smoothness of her skin. "Are you ready?"

"Yes." Her voice was breathless.

"Good." He raised her dress and swatted her butt. She jumped and stiffened but relaxed as his hand caressed her. "I love your ass. Always have." He squeezed. It was firm and round and ripe. He bent and nipped her.

"Oh..." It was a gasp of both surprise and pleasure.

"Like that, did you?" He wanted to shout his triumph. She wanted him. He was making her hot and needy. "Answer me." He slapped her again, a little harder this time.

"Yes." She pushed her ass up in the air for more.

"Then you're going to love this."

CHAPTER 19: LIZ

Liz almost melted as Craig massaged her ass. She loved the feel of his hands on her skin, but not being able to move, being at his mercy was driving her wild. She'd almost come when he'd nipped her butt cheek. She hadn't expected it. She'd never known him to have a kinky side. Of course, she'd never been tied to a post before either. Perhaps, they both had untapped fantasies.

She shivered as he kissed the small of her back, his lips trailing down to her butt. His strong hands grabbed her legs, holding them apart. His breath tickled the inside of her thighs. Oh god, he was going to go down on her. Here. On stage. In front of everyone. She trembled in anticipation, every nerve waiting for his next move. He kissed the inside of her thigh, his mouth hot and open. He licked his way up her leg. She moaned, trying to get closer to him. She needed his lips on her. He nipped her leg, a sharp sting like a bee, causing her to gasp, before his tongue came out, soothing the bite.

"You're so wet." His breath fanned over her aching flesh.

"Please." She tried to shift backward, show him what she needed, but his hands and the restraints held her in place.

"This is my pussy, Liz. Mine." He slapped her ass and his mouth came down on her, his tongue licking her swollen flesh before thrusting inside.

"Oh...god..." It'd been too long. Way too long.

He licked and sucked, teasing all around her tiny nub that was so tense with desire. "You like this. Tell me, you like this."

"Yes. Yes." She was panting. "But I need more, Craig. Please."

He stilled and she whimpered. She'd blown it. She'd said his name. If he stopped now...

His mouth came back and this time it was like he was starving. His tongue pressed inside her thrusting over and over before he focused on her clit, giving it little flicks and sending sparks of fire through her limbs.

"Oh....god...oh please." Her body trembled, so close to the edge.

His lips found her nub and he sucked. Her legs trembled. She was so close. He moved his face, thrusting two fingers inside her at the same time that he slapped her ass. The jolt of the crack made his fingers hit her g-spot, sending her over the edge. She cried out as her body clenched onto him. He continued to thrust his fingers and lick her, prolonging her orgasm and wringing everything from her.

She collapsed, held up by the rail and nothing else. He slid his fingers from her and unhooked the Velcro from her wrists and ankles. He stood. She could feel his erection, pressing against her ass. Her thighs twitched and a low heat bubbled inside her. He'd fuck her now, and she wanted it. It no longer mattered that they were in front of a room full of strangers. She wanted her husband inside her—filling her, making her forget everything but him—but instead of unzipping his pants, he pulled her dress down and lifted her in his arms.

"What are you doing? Where are we going?"

He strode off the stage and across the room.

"I don't want to leave." Once this night was over, they might be too. He may not want her after this. She may not be able to stay with him. She still wasn't sure if she believed that he hadn't had an affair.

"Don't worry. You're not getting away from me yet. It's still Christmas Eve." He kissed the top of her head.

"Then where are you taking me?" She snuggled closer to him.

"To a suite. So, I can show you all the things I want to do to my wife."

CHAPTER 20: CRAIG

Craig couldn't believe this was happening. He had another chance to make things right. Liz still wanted him. Fuck, he'd almost come in his pants at the first taste of her hot, wet pussy. If she hadn't given him the blow job earlier he probably would've embarrassed himself.

He used the key Ethan had given him to open the door. The room was gorgeous and had everything they could possibly need. There was a bed, a bathroom and a kitchenette with a fully stocked bar.

He placed Liz on a big, comfy lounge chair. She looked adorable—her eyes soft and hair rumpled like she'd just had fabulous sex—and she had. He'd given her a screaming orgasm. He wanted to pound his chest with pride, instead he kissed her on the forehead.

"Where are you going?" She stared up at him, her dark eyes heavy with worry.

"To get us some water. I'll be right back." She had no reason to be concerned. There was no way he was leaving her tonight or ever.

She nodded and wiggled, making herself more comfortable.

He went to the kitchen and grabbed a bottle of water from the fridge. He walked back to the chair and put the bottle on the table. He bent, lifting her. She wrapped her arms around his neck, her breasts pressing against him. He wanted to lie her down and sink into her, but it wasn't the right time. Not yet. He sat on the chair and cradled her on his lap.

She sighed, relaxing against him.

"Here." He handed her the water.

She sat up and he immediately missed her softness. He had to make this work. She opened the water. He couldn't look away as her lips wrapped around that lucky bottle. His dick hardened even more as he remembered the feel of those lips, licking and sucking him.

73

She pulled the bottle away from her mouth. Her eyes locked with his as she licked her lips. "Want some?"

He wanted more than water but he took it and drank, placing the bottle on the table when he was done.

She shifted, pressing against his erection and he closed his eyes in bliss. She lifted off his lap.

His eyes flew open and he grabbed her hand. "Where are you going? It's not midnight yet."

"Absolutely nowhere." She smiled as she reached behind her, unzipping her dress.

"Liz..." He was going to say that they didn't have to have sex, that holding her was enough for him, but it wasn't. Maybe, it wasn't enough for her either.

She let the dress fall. Her black lace bra pushed her generous breasts up almost indecently, making his mouth water.

"Come here." He grasped her hips.

"Wait." She stepped back and slid her underwear down her legs.

His eyes locked on the juncture between her thighs. Heaven was right in front of him. All he had to do was get inside. She bent to take off her shoes.

"Leave them on." They were high and sexy as hell.

Her eyes widened but she grinned, putting her hands on his shoulders. She slowly lowered herself until she was straddling him, hovering right above his throbbing cock. He should let her lead, but he'd run out of patience. He had to feel her. His hands went to her waist, pulling her against his erection. His hips rocked upward without thought—only action and need.

"You're overdressed."

"I am." His hands wandered, caressing her waist, her back, anywhere and everywhere. He couldn't touch her enough. She was so warm and soft, silky and his. All his.

She unbuttoned his shirt and he helped her remove it.

"Still too many clothes," he said.

She reached between them but he stopped her hand.

"I meant you." His eyes met hers.

Her eyes darkened even more as she unhooked her bra, holding it in place for a moment before letting it fall.

His gaze dropped to her chest. "God, you're so beautiful." His hands moved on their own, cupping her. She was soft everywhere but these...these were softer than clouds.

She grasped his head, pulling him forward. His mouth latched onto her breast, kissing his way along the top and down the sides, underneath, everywhere but where she most wanted him. "Tell me what you want."

"Please. Kiss me."

"He kissed her breast again, letting his tongue dance along her skin, but not touching her nipple.

"Please."

"Talk dirty to me, Liz. I want to hear you say it." He grabbed her face. "I can't read your mind. I need you to talk to me."

Her eyes sharpened. They both knew he wasn't just talking about sex.

CHAPTER 21: LIZ

Liz couldn't believe Craig was bringing this up now. She didn't want to talk. She still wasn't sure what she believed about him and this Club. If they talked, all this could end and she needed him. If she couldn't have him forever, she'd settle for tonight. "I'm not ready to...Let's just enjoy tonight. Each other."

His face tightened. He wasn't happy, but he nodded slightly. "Okay. For now. But I'm not doing anything until you tell me what you want." He leaned back, a slight smirk on his handsome face.

She wanted to hit him. He knew she had no experience with talking dirty. Well damnit, she was going to surprise him. She reached between them and stroked him through his pants. "This...I want your great, big cock."

His eyes darkened, giving her a boost of confidence.

"I want you to fuck me." She swore he grew in her hand. She squeezed him a little and he almost hissed with pleasure. She should've done this years ago. "I want your dick so deep inside me that I don't know where you end and I begin."

He almost growled as he pushed her hand aside and unzipped his pants.

"And I want you sucking my breasts while you're fucking me."

"Shit, Liz." He grabbed her face and lowered his lips toward hers, but shifted and kissed her neck.

A kiss would ruin the game. There'd be no more pretending they were strangers if they kissed. His lips trailed down her neck, while one of his hands grabbed her ass and the other dipped between her legs.

"Oh...god." She clung to his shoulder and one hand drifted to his head, her fingers getting tangled in that damn mask.

His dick was hot and heavy at the juncture of her legs, but she didn't want to fuck some masked man. "Wait."

His hips thrust, making his penis stroke along her clit.

She moaned. "Please..."

"What, Liz? Please fuck you? Say that. Please fucking say that." He was panting on her neck his body as tight as a bow.

"Not yet."

His head dropped to her shoulder. "Fuck me. I'm gonna die. Right here."

She laughed. "No, you're not." She grabbed his shoulders, pushing him away from her neck. Her eyes met his as her hands touched his mask.

"Are you sure?" His finger caressed her cheek.

"Yes." Her hands skimmed around the back of his head, searching for the tie that kept his disguise in place.

He grabbed her wrists. "Are you absolutely sure? There's no pretending once you do this."

She leaned forward and kissed him. His lips were warm and familiar. "I'm done pretending. I want you."

She shoved the mask off his face and he grabbed her lifting her in his arms. He kicked his legs, losing his pants and heading for the bed. She shoved her mask off before cupping his cheeks and kissing him. She'd missed sex but she'd missed kissing him more. God help her, she still loved this man.

He dropped her on the bed and followed her down, his hot, strong body surrounding her and making her feel safe. He pushed the hair from her face, his eyes dark and warm with more than desire.

She glanced away unable to stand the intensity. They still had a lot to talk about but right now, she didn't want to talk. "Fuck me, Craig. Please."

He shoved her thighs apart with his knee, positioning himself at her entrance. "This is going to be fast and hard, Liz. I won't be able to hold out long."

"Good." She wrapped her legs around him and reached between them, grabbing his cock. She shifted upward, rubbing him against her wetness.

"You're so wet." He slipped inside a little.

Oh, she'd missed this. "That feels so good."

"You feel so good." He thrust his hips and pushed all the way inside of her.

She gasped. It'd been months since they'd had sex. She was tight and full and it was wonderful. She rocked against him, needing more. He took her hint and began thrusting in short, hard jabs that sent her world spiraling.

"Oh, yes. That's it. Please."

"Say my name." He rasped in her ear. "Scream my name when you come."

Her hands tangled in his hair, holding him to her. He shifted, lowering his mouth to her breast, sucking on a nipple, making it so sensitive. He pulled on it with his teeth and it was too much—too much sensation, too much pleasure.

"Craig..." She broke apart, her hips bucking against him and her pussy clenching onto his dick, never going to let him go.

"Liz..." He groaned against her breast as he came, his body stiffening and thrusting with his release.

He collapsed on top of her. Her hands clutched his hair, unwilling to let him go, to let this night end.

A few moments later, he rolled off her. He was close but not touching. She wanted to curl into his side but wasn't sure it was what he wanted. There was still so much between them that had to be said. She'd loved tonight but had he? Was he regretting this evening already? She'd never felt so awkward in her life. If he didn't say something soon, she was going to cry and she couldn't do that. She had to salvage this. "It's not midnight yet."

"The masks are gone, Liz."

"I know, but...it's Christmas Eve. Can't we forget everything until tomorrow?"

He didn't say anything. She blinked back tears as she started to sit up. She was leaving. She wasn't going to cry in front of him. He'd caused too many tears as it was.

"Wait." He grabbed her hand. "Don't go."

She turned to him. Hope flaring in her chest at the look of longing on his face.

"We can do whatever you want, but don't leave."

She nodded and stretched out next to him. He pulled her against his side, her head tucked under his arm and her hand resting on his chest.

"Merry Christmas Eve, Craig."

He kissed the top of her head. "It's the best one in recent memory."

"Recent?" She laughed. They hadn't had sex on Christmas Eve in years.

He smiled. She could feel it against her hair.

"Yeah. Those Christmas Eves getting things ready for the kids were pretty terrific too."

"You hated putting all that crap together."

"At the time, but now...well, they're some of my best memories."

"Yeah." She kissed his chest. "Memory has a way of turning bad things to good."

He didn't say anything. He wouldn't. He was sleeping. It was what he did after sex. It used to annoy her but she'd accepted it. Tonight, however, she was kind of proud. She'd worn the man out. She'd done that, not some twenty-something kid. Oh God, had he cheated on her or not? Ethan could've lied. He had no reason to tell her the truth.

Craig's chest rose and fell in a steady rhythm. She should sleep too. She wanted to but then it'd be tomorrow and she'd have to face the fact that she'd just had sex with the man she was divorcing. The man she still loved.

She sat up. She needed to think and she couldn't do that naked in his arms.

CHAPTER 22: CRAIG

Craig stretched his arms over his head, his body satiated in a way it hadn't been in a long time. He couldn't keep the satisfied smile from his face. Last night had been great. Today, would be great too. He rolled over. The bed was empty.

It was Christmas. Usually, he loved this day but not this year. He sat up. Damnit, why not? They'd reconnected last night. Yes, they still needed to talk but they could do that on Christmas and they could also have sex. He'd seen a side of Liz that he'd never dreamed existed and he wanted to explore it.

He crawled out of bed and grabbed his clothes. First stop, his apartment for a shower. Then, he was going home to his wife and they were going to have Christmas breakfast like they did every year. He grinned. Maybe, not exactly like every year. With no kids around, they could start a new tradition of Christmas breakfast sex.

He left the room and hurried down the stairs toward the door.

"Hold on there." Ethan sat at the bar, working on his laptop.

"Hey, Ethan." He walked toward the bar. "I want to thank you for last night." He smiled. "For everything."

"Glad things worked out." Ethan closed his computer. "They did work out, right?"

"Yeah." He was going to make sure of that today.

"Where is she?"

"She left."

"Oh." Ethan winced.

"It's not like that."

"In my experience happy woman don't sneak out of a man's bed." Ethan stood. "Want some coffee?"

"Ah...yeah. Sure." He sat. Maybe, she didn't want to see him today.

Ethan poured two cups and handed him one, pushing cream and sugar packages his way.

Ethan poured an unhealthy amount of sugar into his coffee. "What? I like it sweet."

"Sweet is one thing, but that is sugar overload."

Ethan shrugged and took a sip. "Mmm."

Craig grimaced and added cream to his.

"You did talk last night, right?" asked Ethan as he sat down.

"Ah...We never actually got around to that." He couldn't hide his smile.

"You do know that she knew who you were?"

"Yeah. I know." He still wasn't sure when she'd realized it was him—before the blow job or after. God, he prayed it was before.

"Did you cheat on her?"

"No. Never."

"Why does she think you did?"

"She found my membership."

"We knew that."

"Other than that, I have no idea."

"You may want to find out. You did something to hurt her. How are you going to make it right?"

He had no idea. "What are you my father?"

"Just trying to help." Ethan stood, walked to the register and opened it. "I hate seeing couples break up because of stupid reasons." He glanced at Craig over his shoulder. "If your wife wants to experiment...sexually, you should help her."

"I will." He'd be happy to do that. Ecstatic.

"Okay." Ethan handed him a bill. "Merry Christmas."

"Shit." He'd spent a fortune last night, but it'd been worth every penny. He put his credit card on the bar. Ethan ran it through the machine and handed it back to him.

"Thanks." He took another swallow of his coffee. "I've gotta go. I have a wife to see."

"One minute." Ethan grabbed a note from the till. "She left this for you."

Craig stared at the paper, afraid to open it.

"Merry Christmas, again." Ethan grabbed his coffee and laptop and went upstairs.

Craig stared at the letter. He couldn't open it. She might be telling him that she still wants a divorce. That last night meant nothing to her. Or she could be asking him to come over, but if that were the case, why did she leave in the middle of the night? He shoved the paper into his pocket. Whatever it said, she could tell him in person.

CHAPTER 23: LIZ

Liz sat on the couch, staring at the Christmas tree. The lights were off and it looked sad like her. She still had no idea what she was going to do about Craig. The divorce, which had seemed like the only option yesterday, no longer appealed to her. Actually, it never really had. She'd just been so hurt and angry.

Her phone rang and she raced upstairs and grabbed it from by her bed. "Hello?"

"Merry Christmas, Mom," said Robbie.

"Hey honey, Merry Christmas." She sat on the bed, almost crying. She was glad to hear her son's voice. She really was.

"We've been skiing and...."

Robbie chatted about all the things he and his friends had been doing. He was having a wonderful time, but she missed him. She missed her family, the noise and laughter on Christmas day, even the arguing between the kids. Life moved too fast.

"You okay, Mom?"

"What? Yeah." She smiled and wiped a tear off her cheek. "I was remembering when you were little."

"You sure you're okay? I don't like you being alone on Christmas."

"I'm fine."

"I could call Tina. She isn't that far—"

"Don't you dare. I don't want her driving two hours to come see me. She and Trevor should enjoy their Christmas with his family.

"Okay, but Ellie isn't doing anything."

"Ellis has to work. You know that." She did worry about her oldest daughter. That girl worked more than was healthy.

"She should quit that job."

"I agree but she's an adult and can make her own decisions. You don't want me telling you what to do, do you?"

"No, but you do anyway," mumbled Robbie.

"I'm working on it." She laughed and then sobered. "I'm fine, honey. Really, I am." She wasn't but there was nothing her son could do about it. "All three of you will be home on New Year's."

"Yeah, but it's Christmas and you're alone." He sighed sounding so much like his father that she had to stifle a sob. "I should've stayed home with you."

She wished those words were coming from his father.

"I would've if I'd known things were so bad between you and dad."

"Did you call your father today?" Was Craig home yet? Was he thinking about her? About last night? Their future?

"Not yet." There was a petulant tone to his voice.

"Call him."

"But it's his fault..."

"Robbie, marriages fall apart for many reasons. He's your father and yes, some of this is his fault, but...not all." She should've talked to him. She should've at least given him the chance to explain.

"Mom..."

"Robbie...This is between me and your father."

"Okay." He didn't sound thrilled.

"I love you."

"I love you too, Mom."

"Merry Christmas and call your dad. Then, have fun with your friends. I'll be fine."

"Okay."

She hung up the phone and wiped at her eyes. It was going to be a long, lonely day. She went into the bathroom. She needed to wash away some of the aches from the pleasure she'd had last night. She could call Craig. It was Christmas after all. She could worry about their future tomorrow. No one should be sad on Christmas and after last night, she was pretty sure he wouldn't refuse another day of no-strings sex.

CHAPTER 24: CRAIG

Craig opened the door and walked into the house...his house. He wasn't leaving his home again without finding out why Liz was so sure he'd cheated on her.

"Liz?" He walked into the living room. She'd put up the tree but it was dark, joyless. Even the presents under it didn't help because there was no one to open them.

He heard the shower. She was upstairs—naked. His feet moved on their own across the living room. He didn't care that she'd snuck out of his bed last night. She was up there—hair wet and cascading down her back, her skin warm and smooth. He was hard and ready. He could put off their conversation until later. She couldn't sneak away from her own home.

His phone rang. He grabbed it from his pocket.

"Hey Dad, Merry Christmas." Robbie didn't sound too enthused.

"Hi, Robbie. Merry Christmas to you too." He sighed. The shower would have to wait. His son blamed him for the pending divorce and had barely spoken to him in weeks. "Are you having a good time?" He walked into the kitchen. He'd start breakfast. Maybe, she wouldn't kick him out if he fed her.

"Yeah. I guess."

"Is everything okay?" He turned on the coffee. He was going to need it if things didn't go as he hoped.

"Yeah. The trip's great. It's just...I talked to Mom and she...I don't like her spending Christmas alone."

He pulled a pan from the cabinet and bacon from the fridge. Obviously, his son didn't care that he was alone on Christmas.

"Can't you do something? Apologize to her or something?"

"I'm trying. I swear, I'm doing everything I can to make this work." He placed bacon in the pan.

"What did you do? Ellie said that for Mom to kick you out, you had to have cheated or something bad like that. Did you?"

"No. I have never, will never cheat on your mother." Now, he had to convince her of that.

"Then, what did you do?"

"I...Robbie, all I can tell you is that your mother and I talked last night." It was true. They'd spoken—between spankings and sex. "And we're going to talk more today." He pulled out another pan and grabbed the eggs.

"You're going to be home for Christmas?" Robbie sounded as hopeful as Craig felt.

"I'm here now, making breakfast."

"That's great," Robbie almost shouted. "I knew you weren't getting divorced."

"Not if I can help it."

"Hold on." Robbie turned away from the phone, talking to one of his friends. "I gotta go, Dad. Merry Christmas. I love you."

"I love you too." He slid the phone back in his pocket. The shower was still running. Liz liked long, hot showers. He turned the stove off. Breakfast could wait. He started for the stairs when the shower stopped.

CHAPTER 25: LIZ

Liz smelled bacon and coffee, fresh brewing coffee. She pulled the towel from the rack and hurried into her bedroom. It had to be Craig. No one else but the kids had a key to the house.

She dried off and hesitated before grabbing a pair of pants from the closet. They always had Christmas breakfast in their pajamas—everyone laughing and dressed in flannel and big, fluffy housecoats. She opened her dresser drawer, staring at the pile of cotton and flannel PJs. The kids weren't home. It was just her and Craig. He might want to talk, but that wasn't what she wanted to do, not today.

She shoved her every-day nightgowns aside, her fingers traipsing over the smooth satin of her peach negligee. She'd bought it for their anniversary a few years ago. She'd only worn it that one night and Craig had really, really liked it.

CHAPTER 26: CRAIG

Craig glanced at the stairs as he put the bacon on a plate. Liz would be down any minute. She had to smell the food. She had to know he was here. He put some toast in the toaster and poured two cups of coffee. It was Christmas. She wouldn't kick him out before they ate. At least, he hoped she wouldn't. She might even welcome him. She could walk into the kitchen, smile and kiss him, her nails scraping gently along his scalp as her fingers tangled in his hair. He took a deep breath, trying to cool his jets. That'd be great but if she came down pissed he didn't need her seeing him hard and ready to go.

When he heard her footsteps on the stairs, his palms started to sweat. He had no idea what he was going to do if she told him to leave. He didn't want to leave...ever.

His breath froze in his throat as her legs came into view. They were bare. So much for getting rid of his hard-on. It was here to stay and waving a Merry Christmas.

His gaze trailed up all that luscious, smooth skin. Her thighs were covered by some transparent piece of heaven that floated around her. She stopped at the bottom of the stairs. She was dressed in a peach negligee that was almost see through. Her nipples were hard, rose berries that pressed against the white lace that barely covered her breasts. His throat was drier than chalk as his eyes stopped at the juncture between her thighs.

"Merry Christmas, Craig. Breakfast smells delicious." She moved closer and grabbed a piece of bacon from the plate.

"Liz..." It was all that came out, the one thing that tumbled around his brain. Every other thought and desire had raced to his dick.

"Where are your pajamas?" She ran her hand down her body making her breasts jiggle and his breath catch in his chest. "We always wear our pajamas for Christmas breakfast."

He couldn't stop staring at her—at all that skin, that soft, moist paradise waiting for him.

"Did you forget your pajamas?" She walked toward him, her hips swaying.

"Yeah." He nodded like an imbecile

"If I remember correctly"—her hands skimmed down his chest, causing his knees to shake—"before we had kids you used to like to sleep naked." She pulled his shirt upward, her cool hands skimming over his hot flesh.

"I did." This couldn't be happening. This had to be a dream. He raised his arms, not wanting to do anything that'd cause him to wake.

"I guess you'll have to wear that today."

Her hands drifted to his jeans. She slowly unbuttoned them, letting her fingers slip into his pants, getting so close to his dick that he moaned. She ran her hand along his length, squeezing and he snapped. He grabbed her face and kissed her. It was hot and demanding and he couldn't get enough. He pushed her backward until they hit the wall.

"Wait." She broke the kiss. "I want to suck your dick."

"Fuck me." He wasn't dreaming. He'd died and gone to heaven.

CHAPTER 27: LIZ

Liz dropped to her knees and unzipped Craig's pants. She loved doing this for him. She should've made time for him instead of letting the kids and life get in the way. He could've tried harder too, but it was partially her fault. Her mistake to fix. She grabbed his dick and squeezed. He moaned as he leaned forward, bracing his hands against the wall.

She ran her tongue up his shaft and around the top. She licked at his precum, tickling around the slit.

"God, Liz. That feels so good."

She grinned. He was already panting and she'd just begun. She flicked the underside of his cock before taking him into her mouth. He tasted musky and male and her body ached for him.

"Yes...like that, baby." One of his hands grasped her head, holding her in place as his hips started to thrust.

She shifted so he hit the side of her mouth. He groaned and she sucked harder as she cupped his balls, running her nail gently across them.

"Stop. Stop." He fisted her hair and pulled her away from his dick. His face looked like it'd been etched in granite and his eyes were almost black with passion.

"But I'm not done." She ran her tongue over her lips.

"Oh, you're done or I'll be." He grabbed her by the arms, lifting her and bracing her against the wall. He tore at her nightgown, baring her breasts. "I need you, Liz. I can't wait."

"Me either. Please, Craig." She kissed his neck as he shoved her nightgown up, his long fingers caressing her pussy.

"You're so wet." He slid a finger inside of her and she gasped.

"Fuck me, Craig." She needed him now, not his finger but his cock.

He grabbed her legs, wrapping them around his waist and started toward the living room.

"No. Here. Against the wall." She wanted it rough and wild.

"Oh fuck, Liz." He shoved her against the wall.

She grabbed his face and kissed him, sliding her tongue into his mouth as he sheathed himself inside her body in one long push. She gasped at the pleasure.

"Do you need me to slow down?"

"Don't you dare." Her legs tightened around him and she clenched her inner muscles. "I want you to fuck me hard and fast. Make me come."

He grabbed her hands, pinning them over her head. His mouth came down on her breast as he pumped into her.

He was moving faster and faster. She needed to touch him, to feel his hot skin under her fingers. She tried to pull out of his grasp but he held her firm. "I want to touch you."

"No." He thrust harder. "Keep your hands there." He let go and shifted her hips, shoving into her again, going deeper than before.

"Oh...Craig....that feels so....good." She clawed at his back.

"I said to leave your arms here." He grabbed her wrists, putting her hands over her head again. "Obey or else." He let go of her.

"Or else what?" She ran her fingers through his head.

"This." He slapped her ass as he pumped into her.

Her fingers tangled in his hair as he spanked her again, causing her to jump and making his cock push in even deeper. She moaned, her entire body tightening around him. He was all she could feel—his arms around her, the sting of his slap on her butt and his dick buried inside of her. "Craig, I'm...coming." She trembled, her inner muscles clamping onto him and doing what she wanted to do—hold onto him and never let him go.

"Fuck, Liz." He bit her neck and her pelvis rocked, her pussy squeezing his dick until he shuddered his release.

CHAPTER 28: CRAIG

Craig's heart raced as he buried his face in Liz's neck. God, he loved this woman and he wasn't afraid to say it. Not anymore. He kissed her neck. "Liz..."

"Let's eat." She dropped her legs from around his waist.

He moaned as he withdrew from her. He'd stay buried deep inside her if she'd let him. She gave him a gentle push on the chest and he stepped back.

She straightened her nightgown as she walked to the counter and grabbed two plates. "Some of everything?"

"Liz, we need to talk." He didn't want to eat. They needed to get things settled between them.

"Please, Craig." She smiled but there were tears in her eyes. "Can't we just have Christmas, like we had Christmas Eve."

"What?"

"I don't want to fight today. I want to snuggle in your arms, eat too much food and have sex, lots and lots of sex."

That sounded damn good to him but not only for today. He wanted that every day.

"Please." She blinked back tears.

He couldn't deny her anything but he also couldn't agree. So, he remained silent as he walked over and started filling the plates.

"Did Robbie call you?" She sat and took a bite of toast.

"Yeah." He sat across from her and folded some bacon in his bread. "Good."

"He thinks this is all my fault."

"Craig, we're not going to talk about that."

He dropped his bacon sandwich. "I can't do this, Liz. I can' t keep pretending."

"Please, don't ruin Christmas." She stood and headed for the door.

"Where are you going?"

"I don't know. All I know is I don't want to ruin today by fighting."

"We don't need to fight. We need to talk." He followed her into the living room.

"Same thing."

"It isn't or it doesn't have to be."

"It's always how it ends up."

He grabbed her hand and sat on the couch, pulling her onto his lap.. "Not if we talk like this." He kissed her neck, loving her scent of vanilla and Liz.

She snuggled in his arms and kissed his cheek. "I guess, we can try."

"Okay. Every question that's answered in a civil tone gets a reward."

"Sounds fair." She shifted on his lap, teasing his already growing erection.

"That's the spirit." He kissed her ear. "Ladies first."

"Okay." Her brown eyes no longer playful. "But first we have to agree, no matter how bad the answer is we don't lie."

"What if the answer is going to hurt the other person?" He hadn't cheated on her but he had no idea what she might ask.

She bit her lip and his dick perked up even more. Those lips had felt great wrapped around him.

"Then we pass until tomorrow," she said.

"Hmm. A pass is going to cause suspicions."

"I know, but it's better than fighting."

"Okay, but one condition."

"What?"

"The other person can't get angry about a pass," he said.

"You can't pass on everything."

"I don't want to pass on anything. I'd rather get this all out in the open so we can move forward."

"I...I need today. Please."

"Then don't get angry about a pass." He cleared his throat, trying to stay calm.

"Until tomorrow."

"Agreed. Until tomorrow."

"Did you cheat on me?"

"Wow. I thought you didn't want to fight." That was his Liz. She couldn't hold her punches, even when she wanted to.

"Are you passing?" There was hurt in her tone.

"No. I'm not passing and I never"—he captured her face—"ever cheated on you."

"I found your membership to La Petite Mort Club in one of your dresser drawers." She pulled away from his grasp.

"I never used that." His hands went to her waist. "Ethan gave it to me when he first hired me. I stopped by a few times to get the feel of the club." She stiffed on his lap and he pulled her closer. She wasn't getting away from him that easily. "Not to participate, only so I could come up with the best way to promote his business." His thumb rubbed the soft satin of her nightgown. "I swear. I never touched anyone. I haven't been with anyone else since I met you." He cupped her chin. "I haven't wanted anyone else since I met you."

"Why didn't you tell me about the Club?"

"I should've." He sighed. "I was going to but your sister had just found out about Larry cheating on her and...I thought it best not to mention it."

"That was years ago."

"Yeah." This could get him in trouble.

"And you never thought to tell me."

"You're raising your voice."

"I don't give..." She took a deep breath. "You're right. I'm sorry." Her face almost twitched with her anger.

"I agree that I should've told you but there never seemed to be a good time."

"Never? In all these years?"

"Honestly, I forgot about it. Once I knew how to best promote the Club I never went back." He kissed her softly. "I had no reason to. The only woman I wanted was at home, my home." He leaned forward to kiss her but she pulled away. "You don't believe me." That hurt. She knew him better than anyone.

"I...I want to but I saw your car."

"What?"

"At the Club. I saw your car there."

"When?"

"Right after I...after we fought. After I said I knew you were cheating." She blinked quickly, staring over his shoulder. "I so wanted to believe you. I did believe you. I drove to your office to tell you that I didn't want you to move out and...your car wasn't in the parking lot." A tear ran down her cheek. "I went to the Club. Your car was there."

"No. You're mistaken. I never—"

"I know your car, Craig." She tried to stand but he tightened his grip.

"Liz, I haven't been to the Club in years." This wasn't making any sense. "Maybe, it just looked like my car."

"It had your business's bumper sticker." She slapped at his hand. "Let me go."

This wasn't true. It couldn't be. "Ben. He borrowed my car."

She stilled. "Ben borrowed your car and went to the Club."

"I gave him the account and his car is a piece of shit. It's been in the shop off and on for months." He was going to kill Ben. The dumbass almost ruined his marriage.

She was frowning at him.

"Call him." He took her hands. "I swear, Liz. I haven't been to the Club, except last night, in years."

"Ethan said you never went to the Club to...to..."

"I didn't." When did Ethan tell her that? Actually, he didn't care. All he cared about was her believing him.

She stared into his eyes for a long moment and then leaned forward and kissed him, running her tongue along the seam of his lips. He opened for her and the kiss soon turned more passionate.

He broke away. If he didn't stop now, he'd never get his question answered. "My turn for a question."

"Okay." She was wary.

He wasn't sure he wanted to ask this, but he had to know, even though her answer might ruin Christmas. "When did you know it was me at the Club?"

"Right away."

"Before the blow job?"

"Craig!"

"I have to know, Liz. The truth. I know you were hurt and angry. I understand you were trying to get back at me for the affair I didn't have." Those words came out hard and angry. He hated to believe she'd been willing to suck a stranger's dick to get even with him.

She touched his face. "I knew it was you when you got up to go to the rest room." She kissed him softly and smiled against his lips. "I was checking out your ass and I recognized you." She straightened. "I even left a note with the bartender."

"A note." He shifted, digging in his pocket. "This note?"

"Yes. Open it."

He did. She had known. He sighed. "Oh God, Liz. I'm sorry you thought I cheated." Just the idea that she hadn't known it was him had killed him, let alone believing she'd actually done things with another man. "This could've ruined us. Why didn't you talk to me? Tell me you found the membership card and that you saw my car. You didn't even give me a chance to explain." That hurt the worst. "You're my best friend. We should talk about everything."

She took a deep, shaky breath. "I...I'm sorry. I...At first I was so mad...hurt. I sat in that parking lot for over an hour, staring at your car and imagining..." Tears filled her big, brown eyes.

"Oh, honey." He pulled her against his chest and she sobbed.

"And...and...you hadn't...we hadn't...in forever and I...I thought...I was sure it was because you were going to that Club."

"Oh, Liz." He ran his hand over his face. Confession time was here. "I was embarrassed."

"About what?" She sat up, wiping the tears from her cheeks.

"I couldn't..." This was not easy to say. "I couldn't...You know." His eyes dropped to his pants where his trusty companion was hard and ready to go. Thank God.

"You couldn't get it up?"

"Yes." He wanted to hide. No, he wanted to toss her on her back and fuck her. Prove that he was still a virile man.

"Why? I mean, what happened? Are you sick? Were you sick? If you were sick and didn't tell m—"

"At the time, I didn't know what was causing it. I had new accounts and had to fire two employees. I thought it might be stress."

"Did you see a doctor? You should see a doctor."

"I'm fine, Liz." He loved that she worried about him. "I did go to the doctor and I'm fine." His eyes dropped to his pants again. "As you're well aware."

"You're sure it isn't a Christmas miracle?" Her hand skimmed over his dick.

"Yes, I'm very sure." He laughed. "I've been able to get it up since I stopped those antihistamines."

"Allergies were causing you to not be able to..."

"Yeah. I had no idea. Luckily, the doctor did."

"You still should've told me."

"It isn't something guys like to talk about."

"I'm your wife."

"I know"—he a ran his thumb over her cheek—"and you're going to stay that way too." There was an unspoken question in his words.

"Yes. I am." She kissed him.

He pulled her close, her thigh rubbing against his erection and her breasts against his chest. His hand skimmed up the smooth skin of her legs.

She captured his wrist and pulled away. "You still should've talked to me about it."

"Yeah. I guess."

"We're a team, remember? We need to tell each other everything."

His hands wandered up and down her legs. He was ready to fuck, enough talking but..."You should've talked to me too. I had no idea what was wrong. You told me to leave and that you wanted a divorce. I thought you were having an affair."

"Me?" she squeaked. "I'm home all the time who would—"

"And you didn't want me to touch you." When he'd stopped the antihistamines and had been able to get it up, he'd been so relieved and so ready to fuck. Then, she'd pushed him away again and again and he'd started to wonder if she'd moved on—had gotten tired of not having sex and had looked elsewhere.

"You're right. We both should've talked about these things."

"And others."

"What do you mean?"

"If we hadn't fought you never would've told me that you like to be punished." His hand cupped her breast. "Or that you like it a little rough." He pinched her nipple.

She shivered, her thigh rubbing against his cock and making him moan.

"Those aren't the kind of things a wife should keep from her husband." He'd always loved their sex life. They'd been young and carefree and then young with kids, but now, it was their time to experiment.

"And what about things a husband wants to do to his wife? Those should be discussed too."

"Oh, I plan on doing more than telling you. I plan on showing you." He squeezed her breast.

Her eyes drifted half-closed. "We did both keep our tempers in check."

"We did." He lowered his face and ran his tongue across her nipple, making the fabric rub across her sensitive skin.

"So..." She was almost panting. "We both get a reward."

"We do and I get to pick mine first."

Her eyes flew open. "What about ladies first?"

"You went first with your question. It's only fair I get to go first with my reward." He put her nipple between his teeth and tugged.

Her hands clasped his head, holding him to her. "Oh...Craig."

"Is that a yes?" He pinched her other nipple.

"Yes. Yes. Whatever you want."

He'd never heard sweeter words. "Stand up and bend over the table."

Her eyes darkened as she stood.

"I have a great, big Christmas package for you."

"You do?" Her lips were turned up in a half-smile.

"Yes, ma'am."

"Can I have it now?" Her pink tongue darted out, wetting her lips and his dick stretched toward her. "I don't want to wait."

"Oh, you can have it now and again later." He shoved her nightgown up, baring her ass. He bent over her. "As a matter of fact you can have it anytime you want. All you have to do is ask."

CHAPTER 29: LIZ

Liz snuggled in Craig's arms, staring at the Christmas tree. It was dark in the house, except for those glorious lights. They looked like she felt, magical and sparkling. She brought his hand to her mouth and kissed his fingers, moaning as she caught the scent of sex.

"Make that noise again." He pressed closer to her.

"Mmm." She pushed back against him, lifting her leg and putting it over his thigh—opening herself for him.

"You're insatiable." His fingers made a slow path down her stomach.

"I want you as much as I can have you between now and New Year's when the kids come home."

"I'll call the office and take the week off." His fingers danced in the curls between her legs. "You're so wet." He nipped her neck.

She turned her head, capturing his lips. She couldn't get enough of this man, but she wanted more and hoped he did too.

He rolled over so he was on top of her and between her legs. His eyes dark with passion above her and his cock resting at the juncture between her thighs.

"I was thinking." She touched his cheek, her hand shaking a little. If he took this wrong...

"Not a good time for thought." He reached between them and grabbed his dick, rubbing it along her slit.

"Oh." She forced herself to keep her eyes open. "Wait. I need to say this first. Ask this."

His nostrils flared but he held still, his cock, thick and heavy with promise, resting on her mound. "Whatever you want, Liz. I'll give you whatever you want as long as you want it with me in your life."

"Only you, Craig." She kissed him.

He grabbed her face, his body holding her down as he devoured her mouth. It was wild and desperate. She almost pulled him back when he lifted away.

"Liz, you need to say it now. I can't wait much longer." He thrust his hips, making his dick brush against her clit.

"What?" She forgot for a moment what she wanted to say.

He grabbed his cock, pushing the tip inside a little.

"Wait." Her body shivered at her betrayal. It craved him, but she needed to say this now. She might not be brave enough in the light of day. "I think we should spend time at the Club."

He stiffened—his back, his arms—all the parts that weren't already rock hard.

"If you want. I mean, we don't have to if you don't want..." Great. He didn't want to. He probably thought she was some kind of pervert.

His mouth captured hers and it was almost brutal as his tongue invaded, tangling with hers. His hands tugged on her hair, positioning her so he could kiss her deeper. His chest heaved as he pulled back.

"Is that a yes?" She was pretty sure it was.

"That's a fuck yes." He shoved into her and she wrapped her legs around his back.

"You're really okay with going to the Club together?" She'd been so afraid he'd be angry at her for suggesting it.

"Liz..." He brushed aside a lock of hair from her cheek. "Last night was great. Fabulous." His hips moved in a slow and steady rhythm as he talked.

"You don't think...I'm...you know...weird because I want..."

He kissed her. It was quick and hard. "Whatever kind of kink you want to try, I'm in. As long as it's you and me."

"Always. You and me. Together at the Club." She moaned as he thrust harder, his fingers playing between her legs.

They were going to have a wonderful life, discovering their kinks at La Petite Mort Club.

See below for a sneak peek at Interviewing for Her Lover (book 1 in the Six Nights of Sin Series), The Voyeur and His Sub. They're all free on all ebook retailers.

Or you can join my Readers Group and get all six books of the Six Nights of Sins series for free.

Click Here to Get Your FREE Books[1]

Here's What You Get When You
Join My Readers' Group

Win Before You Can Buy
Exclusive Giveaways
Free Books
Sneak Peeks

2

FREE: INTERVIEWING FOR HER LOVER

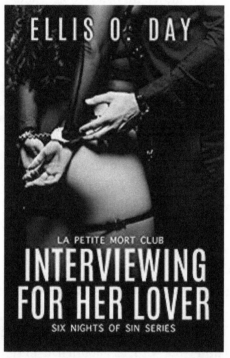

"Do I have to take off my clothes?" Sarah tugged on the hem of her black dress. It was shorter and lower cut in the front than she normally wore, but the Viewing was about finding a man for sex and according to Ethan men liked to look.

"No." Ethan turned her away from the door and forced her to look at him. "You don't have to do anything you don't want to do."

She stared into his blue eyes. Why couldn't he be interested in her? She'd only met with him five or six times, but she trusted him. He ran his business, La Petite Mort Club, very professionally and he was gorgeous with his sandy brown hair, strong cheekbones and vibrant blue eyes. Sex between them would be good. Easy. He was attractive and...not for her. She didn't want decent sex or good sex, she wanted mind blowing, screaming orgasms and that wouldn't happen between him and her because there was no chemistry, no attraction.

"Listen to me." He moved his hands to her shoulders and gave her a gentle shake. "You aren't selling yourself to the highest bidder. You're looking for a partner. One who'll"—he grinned—"turn you on in ways you can't even imagine."

She glanced at the door where the men waited. Waited for her. Waited to decide if they wanted to fuck her. "I'm a bit nervous."

"About what?"

This was embarrassing but she'd been honest with him up to this point. She'd had to be. He was helping her...had helped her to choose the five men in the other room. "What if none of them..."

"They will want you." He touched her chin, turning her face toward him. "A few of them may back out after this but not because they don't want you."

"Yeah, right."

"I'm only going to say this once. You're beautiful and different, unique."

"That's not necessarily a good thing." She had long legs and a nice body—trim and firm—but with her auburn hair and green eyes she was cute at best, not gorgeous. The men she'd chosen were all rich, good looking and powerful. They could have anyone they wanted.

"It's exactly what they want, or most of them anyway." He took her hand and led her closer to the door.

She leaned on his arm, hating these shoes. She should've stuck with her flats but Ethan had given her a list of what she should wear and high heels were on the top. She'd found the smallest heels in the store and by Ethan's look when he'd first seen her she might've been better off going barefoot. He'd met her at the private entrance and his gaze had been appreciating as it'd skimmed over her dress, until he got to her feet. Then he'd frowned and shook his head.

"Finding the right men for you wasn't easy." He stopped at the door.

"Thanks a lot." She shifted away from him, his words hurting a little. She hadn't been sure of her appeal to the opposite sex in a long time, not since the early years with Adam.

"It's not because you aren't beautiful but because you want to be dominated and you want to dominate—"

"I do not want to dominate." All she could picture was a woman in black leather with a whip and that wasn't her, not at all.

"If you say so." He smiled a little. "But, you do want to lead the scene. Right? Because that's what—"

"Yes." Her face was red. She could feel it. She didn't want to talk about her fantasies again. It'd been embarrassing enough the first time, but he'd had to know what she wanted to compile a list of candidates.

"Most at the club are either doms or subs. Very few are switches." His eyes raked over her. "That's what's so special about you. You want it all and...that's what made choosing these men difficult."

He'd given her a selection of twenty-two men who might be interested in what she wanted. She'd narrowed it down to seven. Two had been uninterested when he'd approached. That'd left her with the five who'd see her in person for the first time tonight, but she wouldn't see them. That'd come after the Viewing when she interviewed any who were still interested.

"Remember what you want. This is your deal. You call the shots. At least a little." He kissed her forehead. "But don't refuse to give them anything. You don't want a submissive."

"No." That didn't turn her on at all and she only had eight weeks. One night each week for two months before she'd go back to her lonely life, her lonely bed, dreaming of Adam.

"You can do this." He pulled a flask from his jacket and unscrewed the lid. "For courage."

"Thanks." She took a large swallow, the brandy too thick and sweet for her taste but it was better than nothing.

"Now, go find your lover."

She laughed a little but sadness swept through her. There'd be no love between this man and herself. This would be sex, fucking. That's all. The only man she'd ever love, her only lover, was dead. This was purely physical. "Thank you again." She stood on tip-toe and kissed his cheek. He may be gorgeous and run a sex club but he was a good man, a good friend.

She turned and opened the door and walked into the room, trying to stay balanced on these stupid heels. Men wouldn't find them so attractive if they had to wear them. The room was dark except for one light highlighting a small platform. That was for her. She stepped up onto the small stage. The room was silent but they were there, above her, hidden behind the one-way mirrors, watching her and deciding if they wanted to take the next step—to eventually take her.

She stared into the blackness of the room. It wasn't huge but its emptiness made it seem vast. She glanced upward, the light making her squint and she quickly stared back into the darkness. This was arranged for them to see her. That was it. She'd get no glimpse of them yet. She'd seen their pictures, chosen them but meeting them in person would be different. A picture couldn't tell her their smell or the sound of their voices.

She tugged at her dress where it hugged her hips, wishing the questions would start, but there was only silence. She shifted, the heels already killing her feet. Ethan hadn't liked them and if they weren't going to impress, she might as well take them off. She moved to the back of the stage, leaned against the wall and removed her shoes. As she returned to the center of the stage a man spoke, his voice loud and commanding almost echoing throughout the room.

"Don't stop there. Take off your dress."

She bent, placing her shoes on the floor. That wasn't part of the deal. She wasn't going to undress in front of five men, only one. Only the one she chose. She straightened. "No."

"What?" He was surprised and not happy.

"I said no. That's not part of the Viewing."

"I want to see what I'm getting."

She stared up toward the windows, squinting a little. She couldn't tell from where the voice had come. The speaker system made it sound as if it were coming from God himself. "And you will if I pick you."

Another man laughed.

"It's not funny. She's disobedient," said the man with the loud voice.

"Not always. I can be obedient." These men liked to be in control but sometimes, so did she.

"Will you raise your dress? Just a little," asked another voice.

"Didn't you see enough in the photos?" She'd applied a few months ago for this one-time contract. She'd been excited and nervous when she'd received the acceptance email with an appointment for a photography session. She'd never had her picture professionally taken, since she didn't count school portraits or the ones her parents had had done at JCPenny's. She'd been anxious and a little turned on imaging wearing her new lingerie in front of a strange man, so she'd been disappointed to find the photographer was an elderly woman, but the lady had put her at ease and the photos had turned out better than she'd expected. She glanced up at the mirrors, hoping she wasn't disappointing all the men. That'd be too embarrassing.

"Those were...nice, but I'd like to see the real thing before deciding if you're worth my time."

She raised a brow. "You can always leave." She shouldn't antagonize him. She was sure the bossy man had already decided against committing to this agreement. Disobedience didn't appeal to him. That left four. If she didn't pick any of them, she could go through the process again, but she didn't think she would.

The man chuckled slightly. "I know that, but I haven't decided I don't want to fuck you. Not yet, anyway."

The word, so harsh and vulgar excited her. It was the truth. That was what she, what they were all deciding. Who'd get to fuck her. It was what she wanted, what she'd agreed to do, and as much as she dreaded it, she wanted it. She was tired of being alone. She missed having a man inside her—his tongue and fingers and cock.

"Do any of you have any questions?" She clasped her dress at her waist and slowly gathered it upward, displaying more and more of her long legs. She ran. They were in shape. The men would like them.

"Lower your top," said the same man who'd told her to take off her dress.

She didn't like him. If he didn't back out, she'd have Ethan remove him from her list. He was too commanding. He'd never allow her to be in control.

"I don't know if he's done looking at my legs yet." She continued raising the dress until her black and green lace panties were almost exposed.

"Very nice and thank you," said the polite man.

"You're welcome." This man might work. She shifted the dress up another inch before dropping it, giving them a glance at her panties.

"Now, your top," said the bossy guy.

She lowered her spaghetti string off one shoulder, letting the dress dip, but not enough to show anything besides the side of her bra.

"More," he said.

"No." She raised the strap, covering herself. She didn't like this man and wished he'd leave. She'd kick him out but that wasn't part of the process and they were very firm about their rules at this club.

"He got to see your pussy. Why don't I get to see your tits?"

"You got to see as much as he did." She was ready to move on. She bent and picked up her shoes. "If there's nothing else, gentleman, we can set up times for the interview process."

"Turn around," said another man.

It was a command, but she didn't mind. There was a politeness to his order and something about the texture of his voice caused an ache between her thighs. There was a caress in his tone but with an edge and a promise of a good hard fuck.

"Are you going to obey?" His words were whisper soft and smooth.

"Yes." That was going to be part of this too. Her commanding and him commanding. She dropped her shoes and turned.

"Raise you dress again."

She looked over her shoulder at where she imagined he sat watching her.

"Please." There was humor in his tone.

She smiled and slowly gathered the dress upward. She stopped right below the curve of her bottom.

"More. Please." There was a little less humor in his voice.

She wanted to show him her ass. She wanted to show that voice everything but not with the others around. This would be just her and one man, one stranger. That was one of her rules. "No. Only if you're picked do you get to see any more of me than you have." She dropped her dress, grabbed her shoes and walked off the stage and out the door.

She was going to have sex with a stranger. She was going to live out her fantasies for eight nights with a man she didn't know and would never really know, but she wasn't going to lose who she was. She'd keep her honor and her dignity which meant she had to pick a man who'd agree with her rules.

Find Out What Happens Next for FREE

HTTPS://WWW.BOOKS2READ.COM/U/MLKVJ9[1]

Or

Join My Readers' Group and for a limited time get the entire Six Nights of Sin series for FREE

Click Here to Get Your FREE Books[2]

FREE: THE VOYEUR

CHAPTER 1: ANNIE

Annie finished making the bed and gathered the sheets from the floor, keeping them as far away from her body as possible. These sex rooms were disgusting and Ethan was a jerk making her work as a maid. She almost had her Bachelor's Degree in Culinary Arts, but he'd refused to hire her for the kitchen—too many men in the kitchen. The only job he'd give her at La Petite Mort Club was as a maid and unfortunately, she needed the money too badly to refuse.

She stuffed the dirty sheets into the cart and hurried out the door. She had almost thirty minutes before she had to be at the next "sex room." She hid the cart in a closet and darted down a back hallway, staying clear of the cameras. Julie, the woman who supervised the daytime maids, was a real bitch. If she were caught sneaking away from her duties, she'd be assigned to the orgy rooms every day. Right now, they all took turns cleaning that nightmare. She swore they should get hazard pay to even go in those rooms.

She slipped through a doorway and hurried to the one-way mirror. She stared at the couple in the next room. From her first day here, she'd been curious about the activities at the club. She was twenty-four and wasn't a virgin but she'd never, ever done some of these things.

The woman in the room below was tied to a table, legs spread and wearing some sort of leather outfit that left her large breasts free and her crotch exposed. She had shaved her pussy and her pink lower lips were swollen and glistening from her excitement. The man strolled around the table as if he had all night. He still had his pants on but had removed his shirt. His arms and chest were well defined but he had a slight paunch. His erection tented his pants and Annie felt wetness pool between her legs. She had no idea why watching this turned her on but it did. Ever since she'd accidentally barged in on that guy and girl in the Interview room, she couldn't stop watching.

The man below ran his hand up the woman's inner thigh, glancing over her pussy. The woman thrust her hips upward and Annie ran her own hand between her legs. The man's mouth moved but Annie couldn't hear anything and then he slapped the woman across the thigh hard enough to leave a red mark. Annie jumped. She wasn't into that, but she couldn't stop watching the woman's face. At first, it'd contorted in pain but then it'd morphed into pleasure. The man hit her again and then bent, kissing the red welts—running his tongue across them as his fingers squeezed her nipple.

Annie clutched her thighs together, searching for some relief. Her panties were soaked. It wouldn't take but a few strokes to make her come. She started to slide her hand into her pants.

"Having fun?" asked a deep voice from behind her.

She spun around, her heart dropping into her stomach. "Ah...I was just finishing cleaning in here." Damn, she should've closed the door but she hadn't expected anyone in this area. The rooms were off limits on this floor until tonight and she was the only one assigned to clean here.

He shut the door and locked it before strolling toward her. She'd seen him around the Club, but more than that she remembered him from the military photos her brother, Vic, had sent to her. She carried one of the three of them—Vic, Ethan and this guy, Patrick—in her purse. He'd been attractive in the picture, but now that he was older and in person he was gorgeous. He had dark green eyes, brown hair and a perfect body. He stopped so close to her his chest almost brushed against her breasts. She was pretty sure it would if she inhaled deeply. She really wanted to take that deep breath and feel his hard chest against her breasts.

"Don't let me stop you from enjoying the show."

"I...I wasn't. I should go." She started to walk past him but he grabbed her hand.

His grip was warm and strong but loose enough that she could pull free if she wanted. She didn't. Even though she only knew him from her brother's pictures and letters, she'd had many fantasies about him when she'd been in high school. Her gaze dropped to the front of his pants and her mouth almost watered. He was definitely interested. She dragged her eyes up his body, stopping on his face. He smiled at her.

"There's nothing to be embarrassed about. Watching turns us all on." He kissed the back of her hand and she jumped as his tongue darted out, tasting her skin.

"I...I should go." She didn't move.

"No, you should watch." He dropped her hand and grabbed her shoulders, gently turning her toward the mirror. He trailed his hands up and down her arms. "Watch."

The man in the other room was now sucking on the woman's breast as his fingers caressed her pussy.

"Would you like to hear them? Or do you like it quiet?" His voice was a rough whisper against her ear.

"Sound, please." She wanted to hear their gasps and moans. She wanted to close her eyes and pretend it was her. She shifted, squeezing her thighs together.

He chuckled as he moved away. She felt his absence to her bones. He'd been strong and warm behind her and for a moment she'd felt safe, safer than she had since her brother had come back from the war, broken and sad, and her father had started drinking again.

The woman's moans filled the room and Patrick came back to stand behind her, this time placing his hands on her waist.

"I'm Patrick," he said against her ear.

She couldn't take her eyes from the scene in front of her. The woman was almost coming as the man thrust his fingers inside of her.

"What's your name?" He nipped her neck and she jumped.

"I...I..." If she told him her name, he might say something to Ethan. Ethan would kill her if he knew she was in here watching.

"Tell me your name." His lips trailed along her neck and she tipped her head giving him better access.

The guy was kissing his way down the woman's body. Annie wanted to touch herself, to make herself come but Patrick was here.

He nibbled her ear. "Why won't you tell me your name?"

"I...I'll get in trouble." She rubbed her ass against his erection, hopefully giving him a hint.

"Tease." His hand drifted down her stomach, stopping right above where she wanted him to touch. "Tell me your name or I'll make you suffer." He unbuttoned her pants and left his hand—warm, rough but immobile—resting on her abdomen.

"I can't." She stood on tip-toe, hoping his hand would lower a little but he was too tall or she was too short. He had to be almost six foot and she was barely five-foot four. "I could get fired and I need this job."

"Darling, Ethan won't fire you for fucking a customer."

"We can't." She spun around. She hadn't thought this through. He was her fantasy come to life and she wanted him to be hers just for a moment, but Ethan would find out and then she'd be in deep shit.

"Don't worry. I'm a member and you work here, so we're both clean." He hesitated, his hands tightening on her hips. "Are you protected?"

"What?" She had no idea what he was talking about.

"Ethan makes sure everyone at the Club is clean but only the...some of his employees are required to be on birth control." He ran his hands up her sides, getting closer and closer to her breasts. "Are you on birth control?" His eyes darkened as they dropped to her tits. "If not, it's okay. There are other things we can do."

Oh, she wanted to do everything his eyes promised, but she couldn't. "No, I'll get in trouble. I need this job. I have to go." She tried to move but her feet refused to obey, so she just stared at his handsome face.

"Are you sure?" He bent so he was almost eye level with her. "I promise. Ethan won't care. A lot of maids become...change jobs. The pay's a lot better." His eyes roamed over her frame. "Especially, for someone as cute as you."

Ethan would kill her before letting her become one of his pleasure associates.

"I could talk to Ethan for you." His hands moved up her body, stopping right below her breasts.

Her nipples hardened and she forgot everything but what he was making her feel. He ran his thumb over one of them and she leaned closer, wanting him to do it again.

He did. He continued rubbing her nipple as he spoke. "I could persuade him to let me...handle your initiation into club life."

Her heart raced in her chest. It could be just her and him doing all these things she'd seen. Her pussy throbbed but she couldn't do it. She wouldn't do it. She couldn't have sex for money. Her parents were both dead but they'd never understand and she couldn't disappoint them. "No. I can't do that...not for money." Her eyes darted to the door. She needed to get out of there before she did something she'd regret.

"That's even better." He smiled as he stepped closer. "We can keep this between us. No money. Only a man and a woman." He leaned down and whispered in her ear, "Giving each other pleasure. A lot of pleasure. In ways you haven't even imagined."

There were moans from the other room and she glanced over her shoulder. The man's face was buried between the woman's thighs.

Patrick turned her around, pulling her against him and wrapping his arms around her waist. "Are you wet?"

"What? No." She struggled in his arms, her ass brushing against his erection again.

"Oh fuck. Do that again." He kissed her neck, open mouthed and hot.

She stopped trying to get away. She wanted this...this moment. She shouldn't but she did, so she wiggled her butt against him again. He was hard and long and her body ached for him. It'd been too long since she'd had sex. She needed this.

"Would you like me to touch you?" His hands drifted over her hips and down her thighs.

She'd like him to do all sorts of things to her. She nodded.

"Say it." His words were a command she couldn't disobey.

"Yes."

"Yes, what?" He untucked her shirt from her pants.

"Touch me. Please." She was already pushing her hips toward his hand. She wanted his hand on her, his fingers inside of her.

"Are you wet?" he asked again.

She inhaled sharply as he unzipped her pants.

"Don't lie to me. I'll find out in a minute."

She'd never talked dirty during sex and she wasn't sure she was ready to do that with a stranger. Her heart skipped a beat. Maybe, she shouldn't be doing any of this with a stranger. She grabbed his hand. "Maybe, we shouldn't."

The woman below cried out and the man straightened, wiping his face and unbuttoning his pants.

"Watch. The main event is about to happen." Patrick's hot breath tickled her neck.

Her gaze locked on the man's penis. It was large and demanding. He straddled the woman, grabbing his cock.

"Don't you want to feel some of what they feel?" He nibbled on her ear and then neck. "I can help you."

She may not know him, but she trusted him. He was a former marine. He'd been a good friend of Vic's. He wouldn't hurt her and she needed to come. She loosened her grip, letting go of his hand. He slipped inside her pants, caressing her pussy through her underwear. His fingers were long and strong. She closed her eyes, leaning against him as he stroked her.

"You're already so wet and hot." His breath was a warm caress on her ear. "But, I'm going to make you wetter and then, I'm going to make you come." His other hand shoved her pants down, giving him more room to work. "Open your eyes and watch the show."

She did as he said. The man was inside the woman, thrusting hard and fast. The woman was moaning and trying to move but the restraints kept her mostly helpless.

"Fuck, you're soaked." Patrick's hand cupped her and she arched into his touch, rubbing her ass against his erection. He shoved his hand inside her underwear, his finger running along her folds until he slipped one inside.

"Oh." She grabbed his hand—not to push him away, but to make sure he didn't leave.

He smiled against her hair. "Don't worry, baby. I won't stop." He stroked his finger inside of her and his wrist brushed against her clit.

She needed more. She needed to touch him, feel him. She turned her head, wrapping her arms up and around his neck. He kissed her. It was desperate and wild, but he stopped too soon.

"They're almost done. You don't want to miss it."

She turned back to the mirror. The man below continued to fuck the woman as Patrick finger-fucked her. His other hand slipped under her shirt to her breast. His lips sucked her neck as he rocked his erection against her ass. He was everywhere, and she was so close. The muscles in her legs constricted. Her hips tipped upward.

"Wait, baby," he groaned in her ear, as he pushed a second finger inside of her. "Just a few more minutes."

His fingers were stretching her and it felt wonderful. She moaned, long and low as he thrust harder and faster, almost matching the pace of the man in the other room. She could almost imagine it was Patrick's cock and not his fingers inside of her.

"Oh...oh," she cried out. He was pushing her toward the edge. Her body was spiraling with each pump of his fingers. She was going to come—right here while watching that couple. It was so dirty and so wrong and it only made her hotter.

The woman below screamed and her body stiffened. The man thrust again and again and then grunted his release.

"Show's over." Patrick nipped her neck at the same time he pressed down on her clit with his thumb, sending her shooting into her orgasm.

She trembled and he pulled her close, his hand still cupping her pussy and his fingers still inside of her. When her heartbeat had settled, he removed his hand and bent, pulling off her shoes and removing her pants before lifting and carrying her to the wall.

"My turn." He wrapped her legs around his waist.

Her phone rang. "My work phone. I...I have to answer it."

"When we're done." He unzipped his pants.

"Annie, answer the phone. I know you're around here. I can hear it ringing you stupid bitch," yelled Julie.

"Oh, shit." She shoved Patrick away, and ran across the room, grabbing her clothes off the floor. "It's my boss. She'll kill me if she finds me like this."

"I'll take care of Julie." He headed for the door, zipping up his fly. "Don't move." He grinned over his shoulder at her. "You can take off your pants again, but other than that, don't move."

"No. Please." She raced over to him, grabbing his arm. "I need this job." And Ethan could not find out about this.

"She won't fire you. She can't. Only Ethan can fire you." He bent and kissed her.

His lips were gentle and coaxing this time and her body swayed into him. He pulled her even closer and she could feel his cock, thick and heavy, pushing against her. Her pussy tightened again in anticipation.

"Damnit, Annie. This is going to be so much worse if I have to call your stupid phone again. Get out here!" Julie was only a few doors down.

She grabbed Patrick and tugged on his hand. "Please, hide." She glanced around, looking for somewhere that would conceal a six-foot muscular man.

"I'm not going to hide from Julie."

Get Your FREE Copy and find out what happens next
https://www.books2read.com/u/bxqBMk

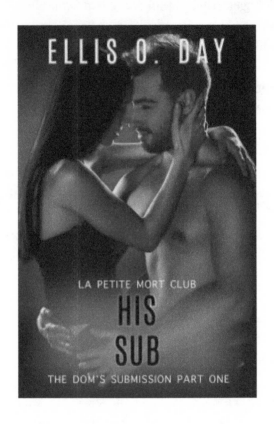

FREE—His Sub
CHAPTER 1: TERRY

Terry wandered through the crowd of well-dressed women and men at La Petite Mort Club. It was the same scene every time Ethan, his friend and owner of the Club, threw one of these events. The members mingled with the newbies, hoping to snag something different or someone interesting.

Ethan strolled casually toward him, a ready smile on his face as he greeted his guests. "Terry, about time you made it down here."

"Like you can talk." His friend spent most of his time in the back office, watching the Club on monitors.

"I've been mingling for over an hour."

"It's your business not mine." He leaned against the balustrade, peering down on the crowd.

"True, but you could sell your practice and buy me out."

"And run this place?" He laughed. "No thank you." He tossed back his scotch. "I spend enough time here as it is." He used to practically live here except when he was at the office or in court, but lately he'd been staying home more.

"Good turn out tonight." Ethan waved at a waitress and a moment later they each had another drink.

"Yeah, but I don't see one interesting person in this crop of wannabe members."

"And you can tell if someone is interesting just by looking at them?"

"I can tell not one of them has an original thought. Look at them. They're all in red." The Club was awash in a sea of red dresses—short, long, dark, light but always red.

"It is a Valentine's Day party."

"I know but you'd think one woman"—he held up his finger—"one would consider that everyone else would be in red and wear a different color."

"There are some pinks out there."

"Same thing, just lighter."

Ethan grabbed his phone from his pocket and looked at the text, frowning.

"Problem?" The Club was usually a safe place but on open night events, when Ethan allowed non-members access in order to recruit new members, the place could get dangerous.

"A little skirmish over a woman." Ethan grinned, his blue eyes sparkling as a couple of young guys hurried past them, almost tripping in their haste to stay close to a group of very attractive women. "These youngsters haven't learned that sharing is more fun."

He ignored Ethan's teasing. He'd taken a lot of shit from Ethan, Nick and even Patrick because he wasn't into the sharing thing. He preferred it to be him and one woman, one sweet, little sub. Since he was in no mood to listen to any more crap, he'd change the subject. "Those kids barely look old enough to drink."

"You're showing your age." Ethan patted his shoulder. "You should find some nice, young thing and teach her how to please her master."

"Maybe I will, if any of them show enough originality to dress in something other than red."

"I've got to go and sort out this problem." Ethan slid his phone into his pocket. "I'll find you later. If you find that elusive non-red dress, I'd suggest we share but..." He chuckled as he headed down the stairs, maneuvering through the crowd like he had nowhere to go, when in reality he was heading for the back—the playrooms.

Terry's eyes stopped and lingered on the new hire, Desiree, who was moving around the room, talking and flirting with all the men and some women. She was interesting—exotic and smart—but there was a shrewdness behind her eyes that he'd learned a long time ago to avoid. A woman like her had an agenda and she stuck with it, no matter what.

Someone slammed into his back, causing his drink to spill down his front, staining his shirt and suit.

"Oh...oh, I'm so sorry."

He spun around and encountered a red dress and breasts—milky white and lush. The skin would be fragrant and softer than rose petals.

"Oh. Your shirt. Let me get something to wipe that up."

He forced his eyes away from those lovely breasts. Her hair was a rich mahogany. It'd probably hang past her shoulders in waves of curly silk but right now it was piled haphazardly on her head in what had been some kind of elegant style before disobedient strands had escaped their restraint. She looked mussed and damnit, he wanted to be the one to muss her.

"Paper towels? Napkins?" She glanced around and then hurried over to the bar.

She was short and curvy—her body succulent, ripe and he'd bet juicy. She grabbed a stack of napkins and headed for him. Her dress was too tight, like she'd recently gained some weight. He usually went for the tall, athletic types but for some reason his dick had picked this woman.

She returned to his side and dabbed at the wetness on his shirt and jacket as if she actually gave a shit about his clothes. This was no subtle caress, no flirtation—just indifferent efficiency.

"I'm so sorry." She wadded the napkins in her hand, still patting at his clothes.

"You said that already." His words came out gruffer than he'd meant. No one treated him with disinterest. He was a rich, successful, attractive man and she was treating him like a child. He wanted to pull up her—unfortunately, red—dress and fuck her right here. They were at the Club. It wasn't out of the question.

Her hand froze. "Oh." Her large hazel eyes looked startled and then hurt. "Sorry. Ah, excuse me." She headed toward the stairs, dropping the wet napkins in the trash before disappearing in the crowd.

He turned around, so he could see the first floor and waited for her to appear. She hurried across the downstairs room, bumping and stumbling through the crowd. A lone, scared, little rabbit in a room full of predators. She stopped for a moment, scanning the crowd as if searching for someone.

"Who are you looking for, little rabbit?" he mumbled to himself. "A husband? Boyfriend?" He grinned as he lifted his scotch to his lips. "Girlfriend?" He frowned at the empty glass. "You spilled my drink. I'll forgive you, but it's going to cost you." He waved at one of the waitresses. "Everything has a price, little rabbit." As one of the best divorce lawyers in town, he knew that better than anyone.

The waitress brought him another drink. He paid, giving her a large tip before turning to find his little rabbit. He took a sip of the scotch, enjoying the smooth burn and his lush little bunny's journey through La Petite Mort Club. She froze in her tracks, her jaw dropping open as she gazed at a threesome on one of the couches.

The woman was sandwiched between two men, stroking one's cock as the other man fondled her beneath her red dress. The man behind her looked up and said something to the little rabbit. Her face heated and Terry's eyes dropped to her chest. Yep, they were a pretty shade of pink but what he really wanted to know was if the color matched her pussy.

She stumbled away from the threesome, bumping into another man. It was Richard, who stopped her from falling and then immediately let her go, stepping away. She was safe with Richard. As a member of the Club and a gentleman, he knew that safewords were law and consent was absolutely necessary. She said something to Richard and continued through the Club, disappearing in the crowd.

"You're not getting away that easily." He followed along on the upper floor, keeping her in sight. He had no idea why but he wanted her. Maybe, it was simply because she was different than everyone else here.

He took another sip of his drink. It was obviously the little rabbit's first time at a place like this but she didn't seem eager to participate or interested in watching. She truly seemed to be looking for someone specific—not just someone to fuck. Well, she'd found the latter because he was going to fuck her. In the office he followed his head but at La Petite Mort Club his cock was king.

She headed toward the playrooms. There was no way he was going to miss this. He sauntered down the stairs, grabbing another drink on the way. She wasn't hard to follow. She left a path of irritated people in her wake as she bumped into them and apologized profusely before hurrying forward. Her full, round hips swayed under her tight, red dress that'd seen better days—hem frayed and at least five years out of style. Not that he minded, especially the snug fit of the cloth, but his women were usually much more put tougher.

They were the CEO types—women who thrived on being in charge. He enjoyed teaching them how much fun turning over control could be. When they were with him, he was their dom, their master and he made sure they loved every second. He told them when to kneel, when to suck, when to spread their legs or ass and when to come. The more power they had in their everyday life the more they craved bowing to his wishes. His little rabbit wouldn't know what power was. She was a hot mess of a woman. Still, his dick wanted her, so his dick would have her.

She was hurrying out of the first playroom when he entered the hallway. Her eyes were huge and her cheeks were on fire. She ducked into the next room and quickly came out—even redder than before.

"Excuse me." He'd offer his assistance in her search. She'd be grateful. He could capitalize on that unless she was looking for her husband or boyfriend. He wasn't in the mood to share. He would, however, allow the other man to watch. He could give the guy some pointers on how to take care of his wife because this woman obviously needed guidance.

"You?" Her eyes narrowed.

That wasn't the reaction he was used to. Women usually purred for him.

"Are you following me?"

"What would you do if I said I was?" He took a step toward her.

"I'd scream. There are bouncers here. I saw them."

Lord, she was cute. "Yes, but if they came running at every little scream they'd die of exhaustion."

As if to emphasis his point a woman screamed in ecstasy. His little rabbit's face heated and she averted her gaze.

"Who are you looking for?" He ran his finger lightly down her cheek. Her skin was as smooth as porcelain but much warmer and softer.

"Ah..." Her breath hitched, making her breasts swell dangerously above her gown.

He could have her out of it in a minute. The skin would be even softer than that on her face. "Did you lose your husband?"

"No." She licked her lips.

There was no way he could let that offer pass. He slowly bent, giving her time to refuse him. He may command his women but he made sure they always wanted it first. Her eyes dropped to his mouth and he couldn't help a slight smirk. She wanted this as much as he did. He moved closer and let his lips rest gently on hers. He'd take it slow, make her yearn for him and then he'd make her obey.

"What are you doing?" She turned her head.

"Kissing you." His lips brushed against her cheek. He wasn't about to lose ground.

"Why?" She turned again, her eyes meeting his.

The confusion in her hazel gaze was as obvious as the hideous dress on her gorgeous body. She may remind him of a rabbit but she couldn't be that naive. She had to be in her mid to late thirties.

He should use flowery words—tell her she was beautiful, desirable—but that wasn't him. Blunt was the kindest word to describe him. "Because, I want to."

"You don't even know me."

He was losing ground. The interest in her face was being replaced with disgust. "No, but I know I want you." Damn, he shouldn't have said that.

"Well, too bad." She pushed on his chest and he stepped back, letting her pass.

"This is a sex club, you know." He followed. "If you aren't here for sex, why are you here?"

She spun around. "I'm quite aware of what this place is and just because I don't want you, a stranger to...to"—she waved her hand about—"in the hallway."

He laughed. "We wouldn't be the first. There are people fucking in the main room."

"I know. I saw." Her cheeks heated.

He stepped closer. "You are adorable." He touched a strand of hair that was resting on her shoulder. It was like satin.

"I'm a mess." She pulled her hair free from his fingers.

"A hot mess. A fiery, hot, sexy mess." He moved closer with every other word. "One I want to fuck, right now."

Her eyes hardened. "Too bad because I don't"—again she waved her hand about—"you know, with strangers in the hallway." She shoved his chest again.

He took a small step back but he wasn't giving up yet. "We can go to a private room."

"No."

Shit. By the look on her face, he'd just made a bigger blunder.

"Let me go." She pushed him again.

Damn. She'd said the worst three words in the English language besides I love you. He moved away, releasing her for the moment. "Sorry."

She harrumphed.

"I made a mistake."

"Yes, you did." She hurried down the hallway but not before he'd seen the look of hurt in her large eyes.

"What the fuck do you want from me? I made a mistake and apologized." He trailed after her.

"I want you to leave me alone. Please. Go away."

He stopped. His little rabbit was running but perhaps, he shouldn't chase. She darted down a hallway toward the hardcore BDSM rooms.

Normally, she'd be fine—embarrassed but fine. Except with all the newbies here, tonight wasn't a normal night. He hurried after her. "Hey, I don't think you want to go—"

"Leave me alone." She walked faster. "I need to find my friend and get out of here."

"Okay, but I don't—"

"Go away." She sounded both mad and as if she were going to cry.

"Suit yourself, but I warned you."

She strode into the closest room. He should leave. Let her find out that he wasn't the worst thing in a place like this, not in a long shot, but his feet followed her. She was his little rabbit. He'd found her. No one else was going to enjoy her until he'd had his taste.

"Vicky? Vicky? Are you in here?"

He stepped into the room, staying in the shadows. She was looking around in the dark for her friend. It only took a moment for one of the six guys to notice the little rabbit who'd stumbled into their den.

"Shit," he mumbled. Not one of those guys was a regular.

Grab your free copy and find out what happens next.[1]

Coming soon:

Go to my website to see all my books and to see what's coming next
http://www.EllisODay.com
MATTIE'S STORY
JAKE'S STORY
ETHAN'S STORY
Email me with questions, concerns or to let me know what
you thought of the book. I love hearing from readers.

authorellisoday@gmail.com

Follow me.

Facebook

**https://www.facebook.com/
EllisODayRomanceAuthor/**

Twitter

https://twitter.com/ellis_o_day

Pinterest

http://www.pinterest.com/AuthorEllisODay[1]

ABOUT THE AUTHOR

Ellis O. Day loves reading and writing about love and sex. She believes that although the two don't have to go together, it's best when they do (both in life and in fantasy).

Don't miss out!

Visit the website below and you can sign up to receive emails whenever Ellis O. Day publishes a new book. There's no charge and no obligation.

https://books2read.com/r/B-A-WMME-VNEW

BOOKS 2 READ

Connecting independent readers to independent writers.

Also by Ellis O. Day

La Petite Mort Club
Six Nights of Sin
The Voyeur Series Books 1 - 4
Six Weeks of Seduction
A Merry Masquerade For Christmas
The Dom's Submission Series (Parts 1-3)

La Petite Mort Club Intimate Encounters
His Lesson

Six Nights Of Sin
Interviewing For Her Lover
Taking Control
School Fantasy
Master-Slave Fantasy
Punishment Fantasy
The Proposition

The Dom's Submission
His Sub
His Mission
His Submission

The Voyeur
The Voyeur
Watching the Voyeur
Touching the Voyeur
Loving the Voyeur

CPSIA information can be obtained
at www.ICGtesting.com
Printed in the USA
BVHW050122161122
651985BV00009B/614